The Duke's Regret

A Short Regency Novel

Catherine Kullmann

First published in 2019 by
Willow Books
D04 H397
Dublin, Ireland

Cover design by BooksGoSocial.

Cover image of unknown Regency gentleman from a miniature in the author's private collection.

*For Christopher, Beta-Reader Extraordinaire, with love and
many thanks for his continued support*

Chapter One

London, March 1816

"**B**astard! Ignorant poltroon! Oh! Beg your pardon, Gracechurch. Not you! Didn't see you there."

"Good God, Malvin! What has you in such a state?" The Duke of Gracechurch automatically steadied the grey-haired man who had almost knocked him down the steps of Whites. "Come back inside with me for a moment and sit down."

Lord Malvin shook him off. Flecks of angry red stained his cheeks and he leaned heavily on his cane, struggling to catch his breath. "No. If I see that blackguard Rembleton again, I'll throttle him."

"Shall we go elsewhere?" Gracechurch suggested, worried that the older man was about to collapse at his feet. When there was no response, he hailed a passing hack and steered him towards it.

Malvin looked around, bemused. "What?"

Gracechurch urged him into the carriage. "You'll take a glass at home with me."

"What? Oh, yes. Much obliged. I apologise, Gracechurch. I'm not myself."

"Take your time. You'll soon feel more the thing."

By the time they reached Gracechurch House Malvin was breathing more easily. He meekly handed over his hat and gloves and allowed himself to be divested of his greatcoat, before following his host to the library where he subsided into a chair beside the fire.

"Thank you," he said, accepting a glass of brandy. "I should not have let Rembleton upset me so."

"He's a cantankerous buffoon who gives utterance to the first thought that comes into his head. It's best to ignore him but not always easy." Gracechurch was joint guardian of Lord Rembleton's heir presumptive, the son of his deceased younger brother, and had first-hand experience of his lordship's crassness.

Lord Malvin nodded. "He offered me his condolences on Arthur's death—very proper, you will say—but had the gall to add I should not be too downhearted; after all I still had my heir and his two brothers, did I not? As if a son were no more than a convenience—an instrument to ensure the continuation of the family line—and nothing special in his own right." His voice rose alarmingly and he fell silent, a hand pressed to his chest. "My poor boy," he continued more quietly. "He was always merry as a lad and up to all sorts of mischief. And full of adventure—wouldn't hear of Oxford— couldn't wait to have his pair of colours. Nothing but the army would do him! But after twelve years, five in the Peninsula, he'd had enough."

He sighed and stared into the fire. "He was sent home to recuperate in '13. He'd been badly wounded at Vittoria and then contracted a debilitating fever. We got to know the man then, face to face and not just through his letters. He was a son to be proud of. He might have sold out in honour after

Boney abdicated but he was determined to return to his regiment, even though he retained a limp. He'd only leave when he was sure the peace held, he said. But it did not last—not even for a year. And then came Waterloo."

He sighed again and drained his glass. His high colour had faded but his features still bore the dull heaviness of grief. "I must apologise for intruding on you, Duke. Thank you for your kindness."

Gracechurch shook his head. "Neither apologies nor thanks are necessary. There is very little to be said in the face of such a loss, but you were fortunate to have had such a son and he to have had such a father."

"Thank you, Gracechurch."

"Another glass?" The duke lifted the decanter invitingly.

"No, I thank you. My lady will be expecting me."

"Are you at Malvin House? I'll walk so far with you."

"Is her Grace in town? Pray give her my compliments," Lord Malvin said as they parted at his front door.

"No. She does not come up this early in the year. My compliments to Lady Malvin. Good day to you." Gracechurch raised his cane in farewell and strolled on.

He was restless, unsettled by the morning's events. The unmistakeable evidence of the older man's love for his son, his grief over his death, his pride in his son's achievements, the way he valued each son as an individual to be loved and cherished, forced him to consider his relationship with his own children. It was distant, he had to acknowledge, as distant as his relationship with his own father had been.

And what of his marriage? He could not say simply, as Malvin had, 'My lady will be expecting me'. His duchess would neither offer nor accept comfort, he thought wryly. He recalled going to see Kemble as Brutus. It was not the great actor who remained in his memory but the actress playing Portia as she pleaded to be taken into her stoical husband's confidence. But, unlike Portia, his duchess would never invoke 'that great vow which did incorporate and make us one,' to insist on learning what troubled him. Nor would it occur to him to confide in her, he had to admit. Would he, akin to Brutus, simply murmur, 'Why, farewell Duchess,' if news of her death reached him? What did that make him?

Even Mad Jack Rembleton, for all his failings, had been a better husband and father than he. Rembleton's children had wept for him and his wife had said she would always think kindly of him.

Gracechurch had enjoyed meeting the Rembleton children. They had eaten their nuncheon with him and talked sensibly despite the dreadful circumstances. He had never shared a meal with his own offspring. He wasn't sure how that had happened. Stanton was almost seventeen, damn it. But he had never requested his presence either, not even if they happened to be under the same roof, something which occurred even less frequently since the boy had gone away to school.

Returned to his own house, his thoughts circled back to Portia. A half-memory of her words niggled at him until he headed to the library. Taking down the relevant volume of Shakespeare, he flipped through the pages—here it was: '*Within the bond of marriage, tell me, Brutus, is it excepted I should know no secrets that appertain to you? Am I yourself but, as it were, in sort or limitation, to keep with you at meals, comfort your bed and talk to you sometimes? Dwell I but in the suburbs of your good pleasure? If it be no more, Portia is Brutus' harlot, not his wife.'*

Gracechurch laughed shortly. Judging by that, he had made a mistress of his wife and a wife of his mistress. But his mistress was dead.

Poor Meg. He still missed her. Her snug house had been the only place where he could doff the duke. Last year, he had briefly wondered whether Mrs Rembleton might be interested in a discreet liaison, but then he began to correspond with her elder son and she remarried as soon as her year of mourning was up. Better so. She was a close friend of his wife and he had no desire to emulate the late Devonshire ménage.

My dear Duke,

Will you give us the pleasure of your company tomorrow evening at a small dinner to mark the occasion of my brother Tamm's taking his seat in the House of Lords?

I remain, my dear Duke,
Yours etc.
Clarissa Malvin

He had better put in an appearance at the House first, Gracechurch thought as he scribbled an acceptance of Lady Malvin's invitation. The aftermath of war had brought its own troubles. The new Lord Tamm had whiggish tendencies, it was true, but he had been a voice of reason in the House of Commons and Gracechurch had no grounds to suspect that would change in the upper house. If it came to that, he himself did not always support the Government. Take last year's Corn Law. That was something else Meg did for me, he thought. She helped me see things as the common people might see them.

Dear Meg. He met her not long after he came down from Oxford when seeking refuge from a sudden storm at a small country inn. She had immediately taken him under her wing, conducting him to a small bedroom where she swiftly lit the fire before demanding that he remove his outer garments.

'No need to be shy, sir," she had said. 'I'm a widow woman. It's not as if I've never seen a man before.' She tugged off his boots before helping him remove his coat and unwind the soaked cravat. 'Now the breeches,' she said briskly. 'We can't have you catching your death of cold, sir. My John was gone in three days of a fever and he was a fine strapping fellow, too.'

'I'm sorry,' he stammered.

She gathered up his clothes. 'I'll dry these at the kitchen fire. Would you like some hot punch, sir? And a bite to eat?"

"If you please," he answered gratefully.

"Sit there by the fire. I won't be a moment."

How kind she was to an unknown traveller, and how pretty, with a shapely figure beneath the grey stuff gown and plain apron. Soft ringlets escaped from beneath her cap. A lovely smile lit her beautiful blue eyes. How old was she? Not much above his own age, he guessed, despite her widowed status.

What a relief it was not to be immediately identified as the duke's son. The silk gown and ridiculous gold tassel he had had to wear as a nobleman commoner at Oxford had branded him as surely as the servitor's skimpy garment betrayed his lowly rank. He shivered as water dripped down the back of his neck. His hat had fallen off as he turned into the yard. He must look a sight. He shivered again and held out his hands to the blaze.

It had taken him some time to find his feet at Oxford. Alarmed by the attentions of tuft-hunters and Oxford toasts who regarded a duke's heir as prime prey, he had been chary of too readily offered friendship but slowly found companions among those whose enquiring minds matched and complemented his own. He made full use of his privilege to attend any lecture that interested him. This was how he discovered astronomy. If he was grateful to Oxford for anything, it was for that.

"Sitting in the dark, sir?" The maid tsked disapproval from the door, set down her tray and went to light the candles on the mantelpiece and the small table. "That's better. It's a dismal day."

"My horse?"

"Jem's looking after it."

"Jem?"

"My brother. My name's Meg." She handed him a glass of punch and he closed his fingers around it, grateful for the warmth.

She tsked again, removed a cloth from the tray and went to stand behind him, gently swathing his head in the towel. "Let me dry your hair, sir. 'Tis no wonder you're cold.'

He sipped slowly, savouring the aromatic fumes of rum and lemon while the palms of her hands moved in slow circles against his skull. The soft friction together with the hot punch chased away the chill and he could feel his body relax as he gave himself over to her ministrations. She began to trace individual, smaller patterns on his head as if reading the map of him—seeking to learn each contour. He bent his head to allow her more access and she worked her way down until she could slip her hands beneath the neckband of his shirt where she kneaded more firmly, loosening the tight muscles.

He sighed and stretched, then tilted his head back to rest it against her breast. He smiled up at her and she smiled back, her hands slipping around his neck to meet at his collar-bone. He caught them and raised them to his lips and she bent and pressed a kiss to his forehead. Her lips were soft and cool. Looking back, he could not say who moved first. But the bed was there and they were in it. It was not his first time, of course; his father had seen that he was expensively initiated into the pleasures of the flesh. But this was the first time that it had been for mutual enjoyment.

Afterwards he lay with his head on her breast while she combed her fingers through his hair.

"I like your short curls. Is it the latest fashion?"

"Yes. It was started by the Duke of Bedford who refused to pay the powder tax."

"A duke? Fancy that. I hadn't thought a duke would care about things like that!"

He laughed. "They're no different to anyone else when it comes to paying taxes, believe me."

Chapter Two

The Malvins' drawing room was abuzz with animated conversation. Although the parliamentary session had opened on the first of February, the Season was not yet in full swing and there was a sense of joyful reconnection as the guests met and mingled after the winter. The tone was different here, Gracechurch thought, more intimate; people seemed at ease with one another. There were none of the usual manoeuvrings for advantage that marked the social and political interactions of the *beau monde*. It was chiefly a family gathering, a fact highlighted by the presence of children; mostly girls. They flitted among the adults like a flock of butterflies in their white muslin dresses while the few boys adopted a masculine stance as they talked together.

"Gracechurch." The Marquess of Martinborough nodded to him and made room among the little group of men standing near a window.

"Martinborough. Mr Malvin." Gracechurch exchanged nods with Lord Malvin's eldest son, a man of about his own age.

The third man bowed and said, "It's been a long time, your Grace."

Gracechurch stared at him. There was something familiar about the lanky figure and engaging grin. "Charles Forbes?" he asked incredulously.

"The same."

"Do you still live and breathe music?"

Julian Malvin laughed. "If he isn't composing, he's arranging and if he isn't arranging, he's practising and if he isn't practising, he's singing or playing or making someone else sing or play."

Gracechurch smiled. "In that case, he hasn't changed a whit. Within five minutes of knocking me down in St. John's Chapel, he had me treading the bellows so he could play the organ."

Mr Forbes spread his hands. "My usual man had not turned up and I had to practise," he explained to general laughter before asking, "Have you kept up your music, Duke?"

Gracechurch shook his head. "I broke my wrist some years ago and since then find the left-hand grip too difficult."

"You played the traverse flute, did you not? Have you tried a different instrument—a recorder or a clarinet? The grip is more natural."

"I confess I haven't." Why had this never occurred to him? Probably because Meg loved to hear him play. He had felt very little inclination for music after her death. But perhaps now—"Do you stay long in London?" he asked impulsively. "Would you be willing to show me how to go about it?"

"I should be honoured." Mr Groves took out a card case. "Here is my direction. If you would like to call one day, we shall try out a variety of instruments, see what best suits you."

"Thank you, I should like that."

Lady Malvin clapped her hands. "I believe the children have prepared something for us," she announced.

"That's my cue." Mr Forbes picked up a violin and strolled to the middle of the room where two footmen rolled up a large carpet. Six children took possession of the freed floor space, standing in two groups facing one another, a boy between two girls. Each trio linked hands, Mr Forbes struck up and they began to dance a reel.

The unusual configuration made for some pretty figures, Gracechurch thought, which the children danced with verve while discreetly reminding a very small girl of her steps. They completed a more complicated final figure, ducking and twisting under one another's arms, and finished to great applause. Gracechurch watched, bemused, as they ran beaming to their parents to claim kisses and compliments and then to Lady Malvin who dispensed sugar plums with a lavish hand before dismissing them with a good night kiss for each.

Why was his home, his family, not like this?

"I must thank you for your kindness to Malvin," Lady Malvin said as he took her in to dinner. "You steadied him somehow. He has found his footing again."

"I did very little, ma'am, but I am glad if it was of some help." He thought for a moment and added, "It must have been especially hard for you, when you lost your father not many months previously."

A tart smile curved her lips. "One cannot lose what one does not have. Tamm was never a father to me—or to any of his daughters. And not much of one to his son, if it comes to that." She shrugged. "I beg your pardon, Duke. Now is not the time to dwell on past miseries."

He looked around. "You have three other sons, I understand, but I see only two here. Is your youngest still at school?"

Her face softened. "Roderick? Yes. He is seventeen and will go up to Oxford after Easter. We shall remain in town until the house rises. I think the change of scene has helped us all."

If Roderick was going up, surely it was time for Stanton to go too? He must write to the Dean. They would always find room for a duke's heir, but it would be courteous to give advance warning of his arrival.

Did he have a home and a family? The question nagged at him so much that he dismissed his carriage in favour of walking back to Gracechurch House. Nominally, of course, he had both. But actually? Would his children speak as bitterly of him as Lady Malvin had of her father?

He had a sudden memory of Mrs Rembleton's younger son questioning him about his father's death. He had not known how to answer and she intervened. *They are their father's children, sir*, she had said. *They have been taught to seek the facts and we attempt to answer their questions as respectfully as if they were put by an adult.* What had he given his children? His name, of course, and the wealth and position associated with it, but that was merely passing on what he had inherited. Had he given them anything of himself? How could he have, when he hardly knew them?

If he were to be honest, he had taken very little interest in them. He had bitterly resented the early marriage forced on him by his father.

"It's a matter of honour, Stanton," his father said when he protested. "Without Hassard, we would have been completely dished up when your grandfather died. I would have had to sell all the unentailed property to pay his debts if Hassard hadn't agreed to a mortgage on very favourable terms. So when he appeals to me now, I feel I must oblige him. He's worried about the chit. She's his granddaughter and heiress. Her parents and brother were carried off last year by some fever and he wants to see her safely established."

"But why must I marry her? If you were her guardian, my mother could look after her; bring her out and all the rest of it."

His father shifted restlessly. "She brings £50,000 now and the rest to come after Hassard's death, including our mortgages. I don't want them to fall into someone else's hands." He leaned forward. "Can you not see your way to it, Stanton? It would be a great thing to have the estate unencumbered again. Marriage need not inconvenience you greatly, you know. You may carry on as you always have. You can rely on your mother to instruct the chit on how to go on in our world and once you have got her with child, you may leave her here."

In the end he let himself be persuaded. Bribed would be more accurate. He had demanded ten thousand pounds 'to pay off his debts' and insisted that he be made independent of his father as part of the settlements. Keeping a mistress did not come cheap, even one as undemanding as Meg. But he was only discovering the true cost now.

Tonight, when the gentlemen returned to the drawing-room after dinner, each sought out his own wife. Malvin had led the way, but it appeared natural to the others on a family occasion to follow suit. And in each case there had been a small acknowledgement, a fleeting smile, the touch of a hand that said, 'I am glad to see you; you are welcome by my side'.

He knew he could not blame his wife for the lack of such a connection between them. She had taken her cue from him. And indeed, in the beginning he found her painfully young, not much more than a child. He managed to consummate the marriage. She had not fought him, but neither had she responded to him. His father had warned him not to expect this. 'Be as gentle as you can with her,' he said, 'but get it over with quickly. Don't try to prolong it—ladies don't want it.' It was only years later that it occurred to him that if that were the case there would be far fewer unfaithful wives among the *ton*.

He continued to visit her bed. It was a courtesy he owed her. Although she had never given him cause for suspicion, it was best if he could assume that any child she bore was his. And she was convenient. He halted, appalled at himself. What had he become?

Gracechurch House was dark apart from the lamplight shimmering in the depths of the hall. Gracechurch preferred to use his key, but a sleepy night-porter emerged from his high, hooded chair to light a candle for his master.

Gracechurch took the candlestick, but instead of going to bed he walked through the hushed house to the small drawing-room. It was shrouded in darkness, of course, and he had to light several branches of candles before he could clearly see the great double portrait of Viscount and Viscountess Stanton that hung over the mantelpiece. It had been painted in this very room, started within a month of their marriage. His mother decreed it should also hang here and his wife had not moved it after he came to the title. It was thirteen years now since his father died and he had become Gracechurch.

His mother remarried two years later. Her new husband was a commoner, Mrs Rembleton's uncle. They lived in the dower house at Stanton. He could have refused his permission, he supposed—his mother was only entitled to live there *dum sola et casta fuerit*—as long as she remained single and chaste—but why should she not be happy? She was a different woman now—had shrugged off the Duchess as if it meant nothing to her and resumed her maiden style of Lady Ottilia.

He stepped closer to the painting. My God, they were so young! His wife especially—not yet seventeen if he remembered correctly—a skinny little thing with a mass of dark hair and big, frightened eyes. And he? At twenty-two, he had considered himself a pink of the *ton*, one who was all the go, but looking at himself now he saw an ignorant cub whose arrogance failed to conceal his resentment at this forced marriage.

She was with child by the time the sittings were finished, although he did not know it. Once informed of her condition he had packed her off to Stanton. He had not seen her again until after Rowland was born.

Meg had conceived at almost the same time, but her baby did not live above a few hours. He comforted her as best he could, but their loss made it impossible for him to rejoice at the birth of the next Gracechurch heir or readily accept the effusive congratulations of the servants and tenantry when he returned to Stanton for the christening.

His mother had instructed him to bring his wife a suitable gift to mark the birth of their first child. He did not make a habit of buying costly jewellery—Meg would only accept a simple ring and a heart-shaped locket that originally contained just a lock of his hair. Later, she had added a few silken strands from their daughter's head. Before she died, she removed it from around her neck and pressed it into his hand.

"Put one of my curls in too," she had whispered, "then we'll always be together."

She wore his ring to the grave, but the locket rested in a locked drawer in his bedchamber in Gracechurch House, together with his unschooled sketches of her and the baby.

Rundell and Bridge had supplied him with a delicate emerald and diamond necklace and ear-bobs, suitable, they had assured him, for a young married lady. Arriving at Stanton, he had had to seek out his wife. He found her resting on a daybed in her bedchamber. When he came in, she looked up from the infant cradled in her arms but did not rise.

Irritated by her silent gaze, he had sketched a bow. "Lady Stanton."

"My lord."

She had changed in the intervening months; she was a little plumper and her dark curls had been tamed and topped with a frivolous lace cap that should have looked ridiculous on a seventeen-year old but didn't. Did she wear it to underline her changed status—remind him that she was no longer a girl but a mother now? He cleared his throat and crossed the room to her.

"So this is the boy?"

She gently pulled back the fine shawl that swathed the infant and turned him to face away from her. "Rowland, this is your father."

Stanton did his best to banish the memory of his daughter's still, waxen face as he looked down at his sleeping son. Summoning all his self-control, he smiled as he gently touched one finger to the rosy cheek. The baby turned his head towards the touch and began to work his lips. His eyes opened, he shot his sire an indignant look and began to whimper.

"He's hungry," his wife said. "Pray excuse me, my lord."

He hurried to open the door to the adjoining room. She passed through with a cool smile and a murmured word of thanks, appearing not to have noticed the jewel-case still in his hand.

Gracechurch shook his head as if to clear it. He snuffed the candles he had lit, picked up the remaining one and left for his bedchamber, a wraith followed by its shadow wandering the dim, hollow corridors. He lived alone here when Parliament was sitting, apart from the few weeks each Season when his wife brought her household to town.

Her presence did not matter greatly one way or another. If their paths crossed they were civil to one another and she rarely claimed an indisposition if he came to her bed. He advised her of any additions he would like her to make to the guest list for her annual dress party and always made a point of standing up with her if they happened to be at the same ball. She never objected if he requested her to hold a select dinner, and in return he was amenable to appearing at those she decided to give. Their lives ran parallel, he realised, not together.

He could not sleep; his thoughts inexorably carried him back to Stanton after Rowland's birth. He had finally presented his gift on the morning of the christening. His wife had regarded it dispassionately and said, "They are very beautiful. Thank you, my lord."

Suddenly it hadn't seemed enough. How should you reward a woman for risking her life to bear your child?

"Did you have a difficult time? With the birth," he added when she looked at him in surprise.

"No more than usual, I am told. When I held him in my arms, it was all forgotten."

"I'm glad," he said lamely, trying to forget Meg's tears falling onto their dead daughter.

She had worn the jewels that evening. His parents had summoned an array of godparents to renounce the devil and all his works on behalf of their grandson and they must be suitably entertained. His wife acquitted herself very well, especially when you considered that she had not yet had a Season.

"You're a lucky devil," his father's much younger brother Stephen had said, clapping him on the shoulder. "A beauty—or she will be in a year or so. Does she come to town this Season?"

"No. She will not leave the baby. She refuses to hire a wet-nurse, I understand."

"It's probably for the better. I remember the Duchess of Devonshire had to dismiss one because she was a drunkard. You can't be too careful with an heir. Have I mentioned how grateful I am you have sired one? The further I am removed from the succession, the better."

Across the room, his wife laughed softly at some remark made by his cousin Ferraunt, her new ear-bobs sparkling as she looked up at Hawebury's heir. Stanton sauntered over to join them. Ferraunt may be one of the child's godfathers, but that did not entitle him to other privileges.

Now that he looked at her more closely, he saw that his wife was a taking little thing and it was easy to flirt gently with her. When she said that she missed riding, he promised to take her out the next day if she felt sufficiently recovered from the birth. She assured him she did and clearly enjoyed the outing. He had, too.

His mother commanded his presence after they returned.

"You are not to make Flora fall in love with you," she said bluntly, "not unless you propose to change your way of life and become a husband in truth as well as in name."

"What do you mean, ma'am?"

"Do you think I do not know of the unholy bargain you struck with your father and of your little establishment in Surrey? Do not turn your wife's head unless you are prepared to dismiss your bit of muslin. Please, Jeffrey. It would be too cruel."

He had been about to protest that Meg was not a bit of muslin but his mother's plea, coupled with her unwonted use of his name, floored him. He returned to town the next day. He couldn't abandon Meg, especially now.

Gracechurch got out of bed and padded over to the sideboard. He needed a drink. Was there anything more ridiculous than a forty-year old duke asking himself what it meant to be a true husband?

Chapter Three

"Mr Shorland, pray write to the Head Master at Harrow School and inform him that I shall call to collect Lord Stanton on my way to Hertfordshire."

Gracechurch's secretary, an amiable, competent man some ten years younger than his employer, betrayed no surprise at this unprecedented instruction. "Noted, your Grace. Shall I also advise the duchess that she need not make the usual arrangements for him?"

"No. I'll write to her myself. That will be all."

"Thank you, your Grace."

Gracechurch waited to pick up his pen until the library door closed behind the secretary and his sheaf of letters, notes, and invitations to be answered. Just before dawn he had resolved to become better acquainted with his wife and children before it was too late. If it were not already too late—was he to fall at the first hurdle—how to address his wife?

He could not remember when he had written to her last—if he had ever done so. Please advise the duchess, he would say to Shorland, but even this was rarely necessary. He did not need to give prior notice of his intention to stay at his own house and the Stanton steward informed the steward here of the duchess's proposed advent. There was no exchange of compliments on personal anniversaries such as their birthdays and here, again, she had taken her cue from him. When was her birthday? He didn't know.

She called him Duke or Gracechurch, as his equals or intimates did, but he managed to avoid addressing her directly. It was the same with the children, apart from Stanton. They called him Your Grace or Sir. Never Father or Papa.

How should he begin his letter? *Dear Duchess*? *My dear Duchess*? Her close friends and his mother called her Flora, he knew, but would she find '*Dear Flora*' insulting coming from him, as if he denied her position as his wife? *My dear Duchess* seemed wisest.

Gracechurch House
31 March 1816

My dear Duchess,

I write to advise you that I shall call to Harrow School on Saturday 13th April for the purpose of removing Stanton from there. It is time he went to Oxford. I recently learnt that Lord Malvin's youngest son, who is the same age, goes up at the beginning of the Easter Term. You will know the family and agree, I think, that he would be a suitable companion for Stanton. His eldest brother will travel with him to Oxford and see him settled there (his father still suffers under the loss of Captain Arthur Malvin at Waterloo) and I propose to do the same for Stanton, thus ensuring that he becomes acquainted with young Malvin at the outset.

Gracechurch lifted his pen and read what he had written. How would she feel at this usurping of her responsibilities?

She had informed him when she felt Stanton had gone as far as he could with Mr Humphreys, their local vicar and brother of the Stanton governess, and enquired whether he wished the boy to attend Harrow. He replied curtly, requesting her to make the necessary arrangements. She had done so ever since. He was not accustomed to explaining himself, but perhaps he should add something.

There will be toad-eaters enough in Oxford, all too eager to fawn on a duke's son but I am very sure that any son of Malvin's will not be among them. I shall bring Stanton home first.

Until then, my dear Duchess,

I remain

Your obedient servant,

Gracechurch.

"Lord Stanton will be here directly, your Grace. A glass of Madeira while you are waiting?"

"No, thank you, Dr Butler. We must not linger."

Gracechurch turned at the sound of brisk footsteps. A tall young man strode into the room and bowed elegantly.

"Your Grace."

"Stanton."

He had never previously offered his son his hand, but when he held it out, Stanton grasped it without hesitation. "I trust I find you well, sir?"

"You do, Stanton. We shall take our leave of you, Dr Butler."

But departure was not to be so easy. They had to endure a wordy farewell speech expressing the Head Master's confidence that Lord Stanton was admirably suited to the exalted station in life to which he was called and exhorting him not to forget the institution which had, if he might venture to say so, played no small part in preparing him for it.

Gracechurch had to admire his son's stoicism in the face of this appeal but after some minutes took advantage of a convoluted phrase to interrupt with a conclusive, "We shall bid you good-day, sir. We must not keep the horses waiting." He gestured to Stanton to precede him, allowing the Head Master to accompany him to the front door to complete his farewells.

A raucous crowd of boys spilled out of the different houses, calling farewells to one another as they hurried towards the waiting carriages and post-chaises. Stanton paused briefly to exchange final handclasps and farewells with two boys of his own age but soon caught up with his father.

Gracechurch indicated the high flyer phaeton trimmed in the Gracechurch orange and green livery that was drawn up ahead of his carriage in front of the Head Master's house. "I thought to try out my new bays. Will you join me or do you prefer the carriage?"

"Join you? I should think I will!" his son exclaimed. "What a splendid turn-out, bang up prime!" He walked slowly around the equipage, pausing to run a knowledgeable hand over the horses and stooping to admire the unusual under-carriage. The horses moved restlessly and he hastened to climb up onto the high seat.

"They are eager to be off."

"Jenkins brought them up last night so they are quite fresh." Gracechurch took his seat beside him, gathered the reins in his left hand and lifted his whip. "Let them go," he called to the groom who released his grip and hurried to climb up behind.

"We'll rest them at Hatfield," Gracechurch said as he began to thread his way through the mass of carriages.

"Of all the bad luck," Stanton groaned, when at the *King's Head* a heavy coach crammed with schoolboys lumbered out into the road in front of them. "We shall be caught forever behind that rattler. The other chaps will be pressing the smacking cove not to let anyone pass."

"We'll see if we can give him the go-by."

Gracechurch watched for his opportunity. Now! He pulled out into the road, the insistent blare of the yard of tin from the dicky behind him forcing the coachman to yield. They skimmed past with inches to spare.

"I had not thought you such a whip! Well done, sir!" Stanton exclaimed.

"In general, I prefer to take the reins than to be driven but am not one of your dragsmen who regrets he was not born a coachman and files his teeth all the better to whistle through them."

"That I can see, sir."

"Can you handle the ribbons?"

"I tool a gig about the place when I'm at home but have not learnt to drive a team, let alone such prime bits of blood as these."

"Let us take the edge off them and then we shall see." Gracechurch eyed the sullen, leaden sky. "After Hatfield, perhaps, if the rain holds off."

This prospect silenced the boy for several minutes. Then he said, "Are my mother and brother and sister in good health, sir?"

"So far as I am aware. Why do you ask?"

"I thought—when you came yourself to fetch me home— she usually sends the carriage—I was afraid—"

"That I was the bearer of ill news?"

"Precisely, sir."

Gracechurch had not thought to be called to account so soon. "You will go up to Oxford at the beginning of the Easter term."

"So the Head Master said."

Was there a note of reproach in the even voice? Gracechurch had not thought to write to his son as well, a lack of courtesy, he now recognised. "I apologise. I should have informed you directly. I decided quite suddenly when I learnt that the young Malvin is to go up at the same time."

"Malvin?

"Lord Malvin's youngest son, Roderick. I think you will like the family."

"How so, sir?"

How to reply? He could hardly say, 'they showed me what is lacking in my own life'. All he could think of was, "There is no nonsense about them. Roderick is an excellent bowler, or so his brother tells me."

"Is he? I am better as a striker. Is cricket played at Oxford?"

"Yes, on Bullington Green. What other games do you play?"

"Rackets—and football, of course. One has to."

"Have you kept up your fencing and dancing?"

"Fencing, yes, but no one goes to old Webb now."

"Hmm. You will need to take some classes at Oxford then—learn the waltz and the latest quadrilles. I continue to fence at Angelo's," Gracechurch continued, "it keeps the body supple and the mind and eye sharp. I'll introduce you when you come on the town, but we might have a bout with the foils while we are at Stanton."

"If you wish, sir."

He makes me extract words from him as if they were teeth, Gracechurch thought. The road ahead of them had cleared. "Have you a timepiece on you?"

"Yes." Stanton tugged out his watch.

"There are five miles between the next two gates. Keep time once we pass the one ahead and we shall see if these are really fifteen-miles-an-hour tits."

Stanton straightened and fixed his eyes firmly on his watch.

When they reached the toll gate, Gracechurch slowed to allow Jenkins hand some coins to the keeper and take the ticket. "Now!" He dropped his wrists.

The bays ran as if they had been born for it, seemingly unimpeded by the new phaeton which bowled along in their wake. Gracechurch felt a lightness he hadn't felt for months—for years, to be honest. But—he didn't remember those cottages. Better slacken the pace and pull out a little. As he drew on the ribbons, out of the corner of his eye he saw a door open and a young child emerge. As the bays veered to the right, the brat darted onto the road, paused to look back over its shoulder, then skirts fluttering, headed straight for the carriage wheels. The phaeton swayed and lurched alarmingly, half-skidding into the centre of the road as the horses yielded to the implacable demand of the reins and came to a jolting halt.

Gasping for breath, Gracechurch took stock. To his amazement, his equipage still stood four-square on the road; his pair, heads down and sides heaving, remained quietly in the traces. Beside him, Stanton clung white-knuckled to the side of the phaeton.

"Jenkins?"

"Still here, your Grace."

Behind them a child's sharp cries split the silence.

Gracechurch closed his eyes for a moment. The brat was alive at least, and vociferous enough to suggest that it was not badly injured. "Is the child hurt?"

"He's safe and sound," Jenkins said. "He's napping the bib out of fright and the skelp his Da gave him. As God's my witness, I thought we'd all be spilt."

Stanton ran a finger along the inside of his neckcloth as if to loosen it. "I too. I have never seen such driving."

"Sir." A white-faced cottager, one brawny arm clamping the child to him, came to Gracechurch's side of the phaeton. "I'll be grateful to you to my dying day. You must have wrists of steel, to turn and stop 'em like that. I'm that sorry. His ma was feeding the baby and his granny hanging out the washing when he got away from me. I didn't think he could reach the latch on the door." He took a deep breath. "I hope your horses didn't take any injury, sir."

They all looked up at the distant sound of a mail coach's horn.

"Better make way," Jenkins said, jumping down and going to the horses' heads. "Gently now, your Grace."

Gracechurch carefully guided his team to the side of the road, alert for every little rattle or unevenness in carriage or gait. Stanton alighted and went to help the groom examine the horses while Gracechurch inspected the phaeton, stooping to scrutinise the straps and the big swan-necked springs.

The boy's father had taken his son inside but now reappeared bearing a large jug and some mugs. "You'll take some ale, sirs? My mother brewed it for the caudle. She has a hand for it."

Gracechurch drank deeply, grateful for the cool, refreshingly bitter drink. "She does indeed."

Jenkins wiped his mouth with the back of his hand. "All's right and tight, your Grace."

"Excellent." Gracechurch handed his mug back and cut short the cottager's renewed apologies and expressions of gratitude. "All's well that ends well, man, though I recommend you fit a good bolt higher up on the door of yours."

"I'll do that, sir, never fear. Godspeed and safe journey to you."

Chapter Four

The inn at Hatfield provided a copious breakfast to which Stanton did full justice. "Done to a turn," he said, spearing another chop, "and still hot."

"I suppose it is a treat after school meals," Gracechurch said. "I remember in Oxford we used to stew thin collops of beef by balancing a covered plate between two chairs and burning long strips of paper under it."

"Perhaps you would show me that while you are at home, sir."

"It would be wiser to supply you with a good chafing dish. Our method caused a lot of smoke, as I recall, as well as singed fingers, not to mention holes in the carpet from burning paper."

Stanton helped himself to some potatoes fried in dripping, then glanced at his father's empty plate. "Are you not hungry, sir?"

Gracechurch shook his head. "Not very."

It was only now that he felt the full impact of the incident at the cottages. Then he had acted on instinct but now that the danger had passed, he began to picture what might have happened. If he had been a fraction slower—or faster, so that the phaeton tilted too far—he shuddered inwardly at the vivid images of the child broken beneath his wheels or Stanton pitched from the carriage to die either under the horse's hooves, or if he managed to avoid them, with a broken neck. He saw himself gathering up his dead son and carrying him to the carriage to convey him home to his mother. He would never cease to be grateful to the merciful Providence that had spared him such a fate.

The landlord came bustling in. "Is it not to your liking, your Grace? Will I fetch you something else—broiled eggs, perhaps?"

Eggs, a child's head cracked like an egg. "No, I thank you. Bring me some coffee and a glass of your best brandy. And hot toast."

The coffee laced with brandy took the chill from his bones. He managed to eat a slice of ham with the toast and his head seemed to steady; he no longer felt he stood beside himself. A piece of plum cake completed the cure.

"You are always on the *qui vive*, are you not, sir?" Stanton remarked as they continued on their way. "You had already begun to slow down when the cottage door opened."

"I had forgotten those cottages when I suggested a time trial. When I slowed it was more because of the likelihood of a dog or some hens running onto the road, than a child."

"I did not see how you could avoid him without overturning us."

Gracechurch glanced at his son. "One must try."

"Even if one puts oneself at risk?"

"Even then. It is instinctive, I think. Could you drive hell-for-leather over a child?"

"No, no. As it was, my hands were clenched on invisible reins, trying to pull the prads up."

Gracechurch smiled. "We all do it."

"When the father came chasing after the brat—he lunged forward and got a fistful of his skirts—jerked him to him. By then you had turned far enough, so between you, you brought the thing off. Thank God."

"Thank God, indeed. Would you like to take the ribbons for a stretch?"

"If I may, sir."

Stanton shot Gracechurch a side-long smile. "Now, confess, I haven't overturned you, sir."

"No, indeed. You have light hands—you'll make an excellent whip."

"Do you think so indeed?" The boy carefully guided his team through the main gate of the Priory, raising his whip to acknowledge the bow of the lodge-keeper before setting the bays trotting up the avenue.

As they neared the house, the door to the hall that linked the original Tudor building with the later, Palladian one opened and two children darted out, followed more slowly by a lady.

"There are my mother and the children! Famous!"

Stanton pulled up with a flourish as soon as he neared them, handed his father the reins and jumped down.

His sister ran towards him, her arms outstretched. "Stanton, Stanton, you are home at last!"

Gracechurch watched in amazement as Stanton picked up the child and whirled her around, laughing. "Well, Tabbie, and have you been good while I was away?"

"I am always good," she said with a mischievous giggle, and threw her arms around his neck. "I missed you."

"I missed you too." He hugged her again and set her on her feet, then held his hand out to Jasper to exchange a manly handshake with his younger brother.

"Welcome home, my love."

"Thank you, Mamma." Stanton bent to kiss his mother before enveloping her in a hug. She smiled up at him and raised her hand to caress his cheek.

The true family that he had so envied at the Malvins existed here, Gracechurch saw numbly. Why had he never noticed it? Unsure what to say or do, he alighted from the phaeton, leaving his team in Jenkins' care.

"Gracechurch." His wife nodded to him over the younger children's heads, her hand firmly tucked into their son's arm and her eyes still sparkling with a welcome that was not for him.

"Duchess." He bowed formally. He would have liked to touch his lips to her smooth cheek, to have her smile at him and say, 'welcome'. But how could he break the habit of almost twenty years?

"I saw you drive up," Jasper said excitedly to Stanton. "Will you take me up with you?"

"If my father permits it. First make your bow to him. You too, Tabbie."

The children sobered immediately and came towards their sire. Stanton is more their father than I am, Gracechurch recognised ruefully as he acknowledged their bow and curtsey. "Jasper, Tabitha. I trust I find you well."

"Very well, now that Stanton is here," Tabitha declared.

"If you please, sir," Jasper said hesitantly, "might my brother take me up with him, just to the stables?"

"And me," Tabitha said excitedly. "I am sure we will all fit if we squash in together."

The request floored him. Could they be trusted not to misbehave? He glanced at his wife. She did not intervene and he turned to his son.

"What do you think, Stanton?"

Stanton grinned and climbed back into the carriage. "Will you lift them up to me, sir? But you must sit quietly, mind," he added severely to his brother and sister, "no larking."

"No, Stanton," Jasper murmured submissively, "but I can climb up myself if you give me a hand."

Stanton obligingly reached down to his brother. "Can you get the first step?"

"Here." Gracechurch showed the boy where to set his feet and he clambered up.

"Slide past me, over to the other side. We'll let Tabbie sit bodkin between us."

His daughter was heavier than Gracechurch had expected, a sturdy weight in his arms. He handed her up to her brother who settled her beside him on the bench seat.

"We're looking down at the horses," she said gleefully. "How high are we?"

"Five feet about the ground," Gracechurch informed her.

"I must write and tell Miranda. I am sure Mr Fitzmaurice does not have such a carriage."

After their previous exertions the bays were quite content to amble slowly to the stables, escorted by a watchful Jenkins.

Gracechurch offered his wife his arm. "Shall we follow? They will need help getting down again."

Her hand rested lightly on his forearm, seeking neither support nor intimacy. "I should not like Rowland to take the children for a longer drive in such a high carriage. Once the novelty has worn off, I can imagine Tabitha standing up so that she can see better or Jasper pestering his brother to give him the reins."

Gracechurch nodded. "There can be no question of it. He is only learning to handle a pair. He did well but will need more seasoning. I'll take him out again next week."

"He will enjoy that. I should be afraid to climb into the thing. I've seen ladies in such high equipages and must always wonder how they manage without either catching their skirts or displaying far too much of their lower limbs."

"I have never thought about that. You could purchase a ladder, I suppose."

"I am sure that would be a vast improvement. No, I'll keep my feet on the ground—or in a normal carriage." She shivered, drawing her dusky-pink shawl closer around her shoulders. Her hands were bare, and she tucked them into the folds of soft fabric. "Spring appears to have forgotten us this year. There is hardly a leaf or a blossom to be seen."

"It has been a long, dark winter," he agreed.

Her ebony curls were dressed in a simple style beneath her lacy cap that was trimmed with knots of pink ribbon. If it were not for her innate hauteur, she might be Stanton's sister but she was every inch the duchess. Gracechurch had seen her quell pretensions with a glance.

He watched anxiously as Stanton negotiated the turn into the stable yard. "Well done," he exclaimed and Stanton flashed a grin over his shoulder, then gave the signal to halt. He jumped down, then swung Tabitha down from her perch.

"That was splendid!" the girl exclaimed, throwing her arms around her brother.

He laughed and hugged her. "Inside with you now. Take Mamma with you—it is too cold for her to stand out here."

"Come, Mamma," Tabitha said importantly as she seized her mother's hand and urged her towards the house. "Cook said he'd keep some hot-cross buns for Stanton. We are to split and toast them, he said. May we have chocolate as well?"

"Hot cross buns?" Stanton called behind them. "I'll be with you in a trice." He turned to Gracechurch and said more formally, "Thank you for collecting me, sir, and for my driving lesson."

"Don't mention it, my boy. I'll take you out again next week, but your mother prefers you do not take your brother and sister in the high flyer."

"No. I should be afraid they might fall overboard at any moment. Once I have the knack of driving a pair, I could take them and my mother in the barouche, could I not?"

"That would be famous," Jasper cried. "May I sit beside you on the box?"

Stanton shook his head, glanced at his father and laughed. "You see what he is like, sir. Give him an inch—"

"Pooh! If you never ask for something, you have no hope of getting it," Jasper declared. "Do you like hot cross buns, sir?"

"It's been a very long time since I have eaten one."

"Why is that?"

"Jasper," Stanton said. "Stop pestering his Grace."

"I'm not pestering him. I think he should come to the schoolroom with us and try some."

The schoolroom. Gracechurch had not visited the schoolroom since he left it for school.

"Do you know," he said slowly, "I would like to do that. But first you must let me get rid of the dust and dirt of the road."

Stanton nodded. "Jasper, tell my mother we shall be with her in fifteen minutes. And see that there is a good fire for toasting."

It was a beginning, Gracechurch thought, as his valet pulled off his boots, eased him out of his coat and unwound his cravat. He quickly washed the dust from his face and hands, submitted to a fresh cravat being tied in the austere knot he favoured, and thrust his arms through the sleeves of the dark brown coat held up for him. A pair of light shoes completed his attire.

The grand staircase led only to the second floor. From there a steeper, narrower one doubled back on itself to reach the top floor, the purlieu of children and the genteel employed such as tutors, governesses and secretaries. This had been his world until his twelfth birthday when he was formally installed in the cavernous heir's apartments two floors below. From his birth he had been 'my lord', first Baron Baldock and later, when his grandfather died, Viscount Stanton, but this dignity did not cause his tutor to spare the rod—on the contrary, Gracechurch sometimes had the impression he liked flogging a future duke. He had seen little of his parents and, an only child, had been lonely at home.

Perhaps as a result of this, Gracechurch had excelled at his books. At Harrow, he had immediately been placed in the fourth form and so spared the necessity of fagging. At school he had had company of his own age and more congenial instructors.

The children's quarters were to the left of the stairs. Shrugging away the gloomy memories, he opened the schoolroom door. It was as severe as he remembered it; a heavy oak table and chair for the tutor and a smaller version for his pupil, too large for the infant whose feet dangled below his chair and too small for the schoolboy who had to hunch over it. Today, the room was even more barren than he remembered. The shelves that had held his schoolbooks were empty and his few playthings had also disappeared. Jasper had said the schoolroom but clearly had not meant here.

Gracechurch felt fifty sorts of a fool. Why did he not know his way around his own home? Because your home is not their home, you dolt, came the dismal reply. He could hear footsteps outside. Should he reveal his ignorance by asking where he might find his family?

"There you are, sir." It was his elder son. "It occurred to me that you might have forgotten there is a new schoolroom."

"I had. Thank you, Stanton."

"It's in the old house. The quickest way is to take the back stairs. This way."

Chapter Five

Gracechurch gestured to Stanton to precede him down the narrow staircase. Apart from May Eve, he never set foot in the original Tudor house built on the lands of the former Priory of St. Anthony, which together with appropriate titles, had been conferred by Charles II on his bastard son by one of his wife's ladies-in-waiting. Due to the exigencies of fortune (the Glorious Revolution combined with a fondness for gaming) the first duke had to be content with this house, but his heir, the so-called Duke of Disgrace, who had better luck at the tables, lost no time in building a Palladian mansion beside it. Once removed there, he left the old house to his three unmarried sisters, the youngest of whom died aged eighty at the dawn of the present century.

The housekeeper smiled indulgently as she stood aside to let Stanton pass. "Welcome home, my lord." Her smile faded when she saw Gracechurch and she backed away, curtseying as she went.

"This way." Stanton opened a door leading to an airy vestibule that linked both buildings. The far wall of mellow bricks where a window had been replaced by a glazed door was clearly the outer wall of the original house. Gracechurch followed his son through the deep opening into a pleasantly-proportioned oak-panelled stair hall with several doors opening from it. He was about to head for the stairs, but Stanton crossed the hall to the opposite door, and held it open for his father to enter the Great Hall.

Gracechurch crossed the threshold, then paused in instinctive admiration of his softly smiling duchess who reclined, eyes half-closed, against the back of an old-fashioned, low armchair, her languid limbs gilded by flickering fire-light.

"Gracechurch." As she straightened, her smile fractured and reformed into a familiar, formal curve of her lips and cool eyes. "Do come in."

He obeyed, circling her chair to reach the hearth where Jasper crouched before the glowing logs, his intent gaze fixed on the half bun impaled on the prongs of a long-handled toasting fork. Tabitha stood nearby, a plate at the ready for the moment when Jasper whipped the fork back and gingerly eased a half of a hot cross bun onto it. While he recharged his weapon, she carefully buttered the golden delicacy and added it to others in a chafing dish. The children looked over as Gracechurch and Stanton neared but did not allow themselves be diverted from their tasks.

A tall, plainly-dressed woman rose from her seat at a table that held the tea-equipage and a chocolate pot. Stanton immediately went to greet his former governess, leaving his father once again trailing in his wake.

"Just two more to go, Miss Humphreys, time to make the tea," Jasper called.

"How many have you scorched?" Stanton asked.

"None," the boy boasted. "You may ask Mamma."

"He has proved an excellent toaster," their mother agreed with a smile, holding her hand out to her elder son as she spoke. "Pray be seated, Gracechurch." With her free hand, she waved him to a chair opposite hers.

Gracechurch obeyed, stretching his legs in front of him, while Stanton subsided onto the hearth rug, leaning against his mother's chair. Her smile deepened as she smoothed his hair back from his forehead.

"Now we are all together again," Tabitha said with evident satisfaction. "Shall I froth the chocolate, Miss Humphreys?"

"Thank you, Tabitha. That would be most helpful."

The child scrambled to her feet and hurried to the table where she began to roll the molinet vigorously between her palms.

The governess looked enquiringly at Gracechurch. "Will you take tea, your Grace?"

"Please, Miss Humphreys."

Stanton collected a cup and saucer and brought them to his father. He went back for the chafing dish and a small plate.

Gracechurch inhaled the scent of toasted, spicy bread and melted butter. The last time he had indulged in such a delicacy had been at Meg's fireside. She had licked her fingers and he had—he frowned at the memory. He should not think of that here. To distract himself, he looked around the Great Hall. With the front door hidden by a large tapestry of a medieval hawking scene, it formed a comfortable enough parlour, he supposed, if somewhat outmoded. A pair of large globes stood in front of the tapestry. Opposite the hearth, a pianoforte stood between two glazed bookcases that held a considerable collection of volumes. At the other end of the oblong space, opposite the main door, large, leaded windows admitted a diffused light even on this dull day. Beneath an upper gallery that crossed the windows, a desk and chair faced two lower ones. A blackboard on an easel was placed to one side. This was not a parlour but the schoolroom, placed at the heart of the old house.

The hot cross buns disposed of, Jasper immediately challenged his brother to a game of Fox and Geese. "I'm sure you shall not escape me this time," he declared. "My geese can always capture Tabbie's fox."

"Can they indeed? Then Tabbie shall come and watch me play. And if you beat me, you shall be the fox." Stanton held out his hand to his sister as he spoke. "Come and help me find the board and pieces, pet."

"Miss Humphreys, please ring for them to clear and light the lamps."

The governess complied with the duchess's request and then, with a murmured excuse, left the room. The children had retreated to under the gallery and Gracechurch was, to all intents and purposes, alone with his wife. When had they last sat together like this, either side of the fire? Had they ever done so?

"These old chairs are very comfortable," he remarked.

"Yes. They were in the old library. They must have been made for gentlemen rather than ladies, for you cannot lean back in hoops. That is why they developed the narrow, wide settees, I suppose."

"Today's styles are easier to manage, I imagine and more becoming too. But you never had to wear hoops."

"Apart from court, no." She finished her tea and set the cup down. "When do you propose to leave for Oxford?"

"On the twenty-third. Shorland will go up next week to look for suitable rooms for Stanton."

"I see. Shall you return for May Eve?"

"Certainly."

May Day was one of the most important days in the Stanton calendar. The May Fair dated back to the reign of Edward Longshanks and everyone—tenants, estate workers, cottagers, and villagers danced around the maypole and made merry from dawn to dusk while the neighbouring gentry were also invited to spend May Eve at the Priory. It was the one time in the year when Gracechurch made a point of being at Stanton. He ensured he visited each of his properties at least once a year, so that his tenants had the opportunity to speak personally to him. Perhaps he should suggest his wife accompany him on one or two of these journeys.

Before he could say anything, she continued, "Now that he has left school, Stanton should remove to the heir's apartments. There was not time enough to refurbish them for today, but all will be finished by the start of the long vacation."

"When did you install the schoolroom here?"

"The year after your father died—at the same time as your mother removed to the dower house and we took over the duke's and duchess's apartments."

We, she said, but he was rarely in residence.

Tabitha left her brothers to their game and came to stand beside her mother's chair. "Mamma only goes to the duchess's apartments when you come. Usually, she stays here with us."

She drifted away again. Her father stared after her, dumbfounded, her words echoing in his heart. *She only goes to the duchess's apartments when you come.* His wife had created a separate home here, in the old house, from which he was excluded. 'Why are you so resentful?' a mocking, internal voice asked. 'What of your home with Meg?'

He glanced at Flora who gazed back impassively; clearly she had no intention of responding to Tabitha's remark. And what grounds had he for complaint? That she slept in a different room when he was absent?

The clock struck four. Tabitha jumped. "I must finish my practice, but," she came to whisper in her mother's ear, "may I play the sonatina and not the new piece Mr Bolton set me yesterday? I don't want to make too many mistakes when his Grace is here."

Flora nodded. "First the sonatina, then the rondo you learned before that. If you make a mistake, don't stop and start again but keep going. This is a good opportunity to practise playing before a guest."

Gracechurch had been about to depart but apparently Tabitha expected him to stay and hear her play—as a guest. She played surprisingly well. Was that usual for a girl of her age or was she exceptional? When she reached the end of the sonatina, he applauded and she rewarded him with a beaming smile before embarking on a sprightly rondo that lifted his spirits.

"Thank you, my dear, that was excellently done," he said when she finished. "I shall look forward to hearing you play again, but now I must take my leave of you."

She slipped from the piano stool and curtsied gravely. "Thank you, your Grace."

He sketched a bow to his wife and daughter and made his escape.

Chapter Six

The door thudded closed behind Gracechurch, startling Flora and causing the boys to look up from their game.

"Is the duke angry?" Tabitha asked. "Why did he slam the door?"

"I don't think he meant to. You did very well, sweeting."

"I made one mistake."

"That difficult passage at the end of the first movement? I noticed because I know the piece but I doubt if anyone else did—you covered it up very well. Why don't you run through that section again now?"

Tabitha returned happily to the pianoforte. She had meant no harm by her earlier comment, Flora knew. She was at an age when she enjoyed setting things right but did not yet have sufficient discretion to recognise that some things were better left unsaid.

Flora looked into the glowing heart of the fire. She supposed she should be grateful that Gracechurch finally took an interest in his heir, but his casual assumption of authority in removing Stanton from Harrow had irked her considerably. Would his interest extend to the other children? Jasper would leave for Harrow in the autumn. Tabitha was only nine—she would be at home for at least another ten years. She would not bring her out until she was eighteen and would oppose any talk of marriage before she was twenty-one. But supposing she were not there to guide her? She shivered suddenly. Who would look after her daughter then?

Gracechurch's father had dropped dead in the small drawing-room one evening after dinner, swaying suddenly before slipping sideways to the floor with a surprised sigh, dead before either his wife or daughter-in-law could reach him. A rider had left at daybreak for London but it was another two days before the new duke returned home. Flora had never sought an explanation for this delay. By the time he arrived, she and her mother-in-law had come to an agreement. They would act jointly during the year of mourning, taking advantage of the seclusion to prepare Flora for her new position. At its end, the dowager duchess would retire to the dower house.

"I am very happy to do so," she had said. "Stanton is a chilly place, built for splendour rather than comfort. My father-in-law almost bankrupted himself paying for it. It was your grandfather who saved us—I have never known why. He cannot have been farsighted enough—" She had stopped abruptly.

"To know that a day would come when he wished to purchase a bridegroom for his granddaughter?" Flora finished bitterly.

"My dear! You must not say that."

"Why not? It is the truth. Remember, I was his heiress—all his personal papers came to me, including his copy of my marriage settlement. Your son was dearly bought, ma'am."

The dowager sighed. "I cannot deny it. I was against the marriage—I thought you both too young, but my husband was adamant. Your grandfather was determined on a splendid match for you, he said. He was in a hurry—he knew the end was near and he wanted to see you suitably established. If we refused him, he would look elsewhere, he said—and our mortgages would go with you. Who knows where they—and you—would have ended up? In the end, I thought it for the best. I could wish my son were more attentive to you, Flora, but I do not think he is unkind or cruel, as a different husband might have been."

"No."

Her mother-in-law patted her hand. "You must make the best of your life, my dear. If he is seldom here, he is less likely to interfere. You are the duchess now. Take up the reins and start thinking about the changes you would like to make. You will have considerably more funds at your disposal than I had."

Flora had taken the dowager's admonition to heart. That was the week she learnt to 'don the duchess' as she put it to herself. The severe black of mourning made her look older, as did a more austere hairstyle crowned by a black silk cap discreetly trimmed with black lace. She learnt to mask her shyness with a cool reserve, and supporting and supported by the dowager duchess, took her place at the head of the great household. Preparations for the funeral were in train by the time her husband made his appearance. He spent most of his time closeted with secretaries, stewards and sundry men of business, emerging from the library only to greet the more important of the guests who came to attend the obsequies.

He had remained at the Priory for a full month but she saw him only at dinner and when he came to her bedroom. She knew now what to do, pulling up her nightdress and spreading her legs so that he could take her easily. On their wedding night, he had kissed her, putting his tongue into her mouth, but she soon resolved to turn her head away. A kiss was a sign of affection and there was no affection between them. He greeted his mother with a formal kiss on the cheek, but never his wife and she would not allow at night what was not offered during the day. He was never anything other than scrupulously polite, treating her with the same cool courtesy that he accorded everyone, as if his politeness was something he owed to himself rather than to others.

Prior to the duke's death, she kept chiefly to her own rooms and the nursery, joining her parents-in-law for dinner if they were in residence, but during that month, accompanied by the housekeeper, she inspected every room at Stanton to emphasise her new position as mistress of the great house. She had never liked it. The vast formal rooms were stiff and unwelcoming. Even the small drawing and dining rooms could easily accommodate twenty people, and Flora had spent too many months on her own while the duke and duchess were in town for the parliamentary sessions and their heir was Heaven knew where. It had been her own choice, she knew; she had shocked her mother-in-law by declining the services of the wet nurse who had been engaged for her but in the end the older woman had shrugged and let her be.

The instant she set foot in the old house, she felt at home. Instead of cold marble and pale stucco, here was oak panelling, gleaming softly with the polish of over two centuries. These faded crimson and gold hangings were more pleasing than the icy blues and silver favoured by the previous duchesses, chosen perhaps to flatter powdered hair. The three maiden sisters who last lived there had left their traces—a work-table here, a shelf of books there, and innumerable little artefacts, clearly the work of talented hands and countless hours. Pretty embroideries, charming watercolours, beautiful shell work decorated the walls and filled drawers and albums. Flora's favourites were the exquisite depictions of flowers painstakingly fashioned from a myriad of particles of paper in all shades and colours. She was sorry she had not had the opportunity of learning the art from their creator.

The ducal apartments were a floor below those set aside for Lord and Lady Stanton, and two floors away from the nursery and schoolroom—too far, she decided. After Gracechurch had left and she began to hope she was increasing again, Flora resolved to move to the old house. She wrote to Miss Humphreys, who had been her own governess, to enquire if she would be willing to come and teach her children. She need no longer be alone.

Her hopes of another child had been dashed—it was to be eighteen months before Jasper was born—but she put the mourning period to good use, refurbishing not only the old house but also the dower house. She didn't know when she had decided to keep the old house private from her husband. It had not been a conscious decision—she simply had not volunteered any information and he never enquired about the life she led during his absences. He never sought out the nursery or schoolroom, and soon it was accepted by the household that the duchess's bedchamber was occupied only when the duke made one of his infrequent visits. On these occasions, Miss Humphreys brought the children who were out of leading-strings to the drawing-room for an hour before dinner and sometimes the duke joined them but he never engaged with them, unlike the late Mr Rembleton who had got down on his hands and knees the first time he met the four-year-old Stanton and earnestly advised him on the desirability of separating predators and non-predators as they waited to go into Noah's Ark.

A large log collapsed in the hearth, sending up new flames and sparks and recalling Flora from the past. Now he had come to the schoolroom. Her defences had been breached; her refuge was no longer inviolate. This house was hers, hers and her children's. When she crossed to the main house, it was as if she stepped onto the stage—her Grace, the Duchess of Gracechurch makes her entrance—but here she was neither duchess nor consort but Flora Hassard. Her husband had never before intruded. Why did it matter so much that he had?

When the boys finished their game, Stanton rejected Jasper's plea for another. "Let me talk to my mother," he said, coming to sit in his father's chair.

He took after the FitzCharles, tall and broad-shouldered, with hazel eyes and mid-brown hair shot through with auburn lights. Jasper had the same colouring but Tabitha took after her mother, with dark curls and blue eyes framed by dark brows and lashes.

"And so you are no longer a schoolboy," Flora remarked.

"No. It was a trifle sudden, but I would not have returned after the summer in any case. Do you know these Malvins my father spoke of?"

"Yes. Lady Malvin is the eldest daughter of the late Lord Tamm and considerably older than her only brother. I am quite well acquainted with her sister-in-law, the present Lady

Tamm who is about the same age as Lady Malvin's son Matthew. There is a pretty daughter who has had two or three Seasons. Last year was interrupted by the deaths first of her grandfather and then her brother at Waterloo. I have never met the youngest son, who is to go up with you. Are any of your school-fellows going up next term?"

"Not immediately, as far as I know. I own I should prefer it if I were already acquainted with more of the chaps. My father says I shall have to beware of toad-eaters and leeches."

Flora raised an eyebrow. "Did he explain the difference?"

"Toad-eaters will court the duke's son in the hope of gaining future favours and leeches will expect him always to stand the nonsense. Some men do both," Stanton replied readily.

"That is very succinct."

"I asked how I am to avoid them and he said to stick with my own kind, by which he meant peers and sons of peers. Avoid commoners."

"And?" Flora prompted.

"I don't wish to limit myself so."

"It is wise to avoid those who gush or fawn or are too obsequious, but if you follow your interests, surely you will meet other serious-minded men?"

"That is what I want to do. A university is supposed to be a place of learning. I would like to explore natural philosophy; remember how Mr Rembleton used to show us things and encourage us to think and to ask questions."

"Have you said any of this to your father?"

"No."

"I think you must, Stanton, for I cannot advise you on it."

All was changing, Flora thought drearily, as she sat at her mirror in the duchess's dressing-room while her maid pinned up her hair. Stanton was now a man. Jasper would go to Harrow in the autumn. She would see him for at most twelve weeks each year and every time he returned he would have grown a little bit further away from her. Tabbie would miss him. Would she think it unfair that she was left behind? She must talk to Olivia about it. Miranda would face the same fate, although Samuel was younger than Jasper, of course.

Olivia. That was the worst change of all. They had been firm friends since that first evening when the young duchess invited the even younger Mrs Rembleton and her new husband to dine at Gracechurch House. Olivia was the first young bride she had befriended. Now she was again a bride, but no longer in need of support. Flora did not grudge the new Mrs Fitzmaurice her happiness, but she felt strangely bereft. For over ten years, Olivia and her children had spent several weeks each year as Flora's guests at Gracechurch House. Together the ladies faced the Season while the children explored London, sometimes with their governesses, sometimes with their mothers, and occasionally, with Mr Rembleton who had turned every outing into a fascinating investigation into the wonders of nature.

But this year, Mr Fitzmaurice had taken a house in Sloane Square for his new family. Flora and Olivia would meet frequently, of course, but there would no longer be the comfortable cozes over breakfast or the impromptu games of bat and ball in the square with the children.

Once again, her world had crumbled around her. *Until death do you part*. At sixteen, she had had no idea what the words truly meant. She was now married longer than she had been single and was not yet thirty-five. She did not wish Gracechurch ill, but if only there were some way they could part amicably, each free to lead their own lives. Her marriage settlements provided for generous pin-money and an equally generous jointure. If only she could take what was due to her and set up her own establishment. Would Gracechurch agree to it? He had his two sons, after all, and surely enough of her money.

The door from her bedroom opened to admit her husband. Now he intruded here! She made no sign that she had seen him but sat composedly while her maid set a little turban of ruby satin ornamented with pearls on her dark curls before holding up a mirror so that her mistress could view the effect from behind. At Flora's nod, she curtsied and withdrew.

Chapter Seven

"Yes, Gracechurch?"

Her husband reddened slightly at Flora's acerbic tone but he came forward to stand in front of her. "I should like to talk to you without fear of interruption."

She could not recall his ever having sought her out like this. When they were under the same roof, whatever they needed to say to each other was usually said during or after dinner. If they were separated, they wrote or had a secretary write a letter. What could be so important and so private that he came to her dressing-room, and at this hour?

She moved to a small armchair and gestured to the one beside it. "Please be seated."

"Thank you."

As usual, he was immaculately turned out. He had never subscribed to Mr Brummel's dictum that a gentleman should dress in black and white only, and wore black trousers strapped under his shoes and a coat of russet-brown superfine that looked well over a waistcoat of ivory and gold silk. His linen was pristine as always and his only ornaments a seal ring and three understated fobs. He took his time seating himself, flipping his coattails so as not to crush them and gently pulling at the knees of his trousers. Once settled, he looked steadily at her.

"I have come to beg your pardon, Flora."

She didn't know what nonplussed her more—his statement or his use of her name. The last time she heard it on his lips had been during their marriage ceremony. "What? I mean, why? I mean—are you feeling quite the thing, Gracechurch?"

"I beg your pardon?"

This was the chilly Gracechurch she knew. Her old nurse used to speak of changelings; a child left by the fairies in the place of a human one they had spirited away. Was there such a thing as an adult changeling? She pressed her hand to her lips to conceal her smile.

"Flora?"

"I'm sorry. I suddenly wondered if a fetch sat opposite me."

"A fetch?"

"A double—my nurse used to tell me stories—generally it was a portent of death, especially if one saw oneself."

His fleeting grin surprised her. "So I should not look in a mirror? No, it is I. See for yourself."

She had never voluntarily touched him skin to skin, nor had he ever solicited her touch. She took a breath and carefully laid her fingertips on his outstretched palm. His hand closed firmly as he bent and kissed them. This was no courtly gesture, more implied than real; his cool lips lingered on her hand. Annoyed, she tugged it free.

"If you seek to amuse yourself, Duke, I suggest you look elsewhere."

"Flora! I beg you—I'm not—I mean, I want—"

He shook his head, stood abruptly and strode to the window, where he jerked the curtain aside to peer into the twilit garden below. After a few moments, he let the heavy, pink-and-plum-striped damask fall and turned as precisely as any guardsman to face her again.

"I am aware that I have been inconsiderate, even negligent, both as a husband and a father. I wish to make amends."

Her mouth fell open. "Gracechurch, are you sure you are quite well? Have you seen a physician lately?"

"What? No." There was that glimmer of amusement again. "This is not remorse in the face of death."

"Then what is it?

He shrugged. "A sudden insight, I suppose."

She didn't know what to say. She must have looked pale for he laughed abruptly and removed the stopper from the decanter on the table. He sniffed the contents suspiciously. "What is this?"

"Olivia's orange wine. She makes it every year according to her mother's recipe and sends me some."

"Hmm." He poured a glass and handed it to her, then filled another for himself. "Not too bad, I suppose."

Flora eyed her husband warily but sipped the aromatic cordial. What was going to come next? She glanced at the ormolu clock on the mantelpiece. "We must go down. It is Stanton's first time to dine with us. Your mother and Mr Harte join us."

"Very well." He stood and offered her his arm. "May we continue this later?" When she hesitated, he said softly, "Please, Flora."

With Mr Shorland, they were six at dinner. Flora was grateful for the extra company. Her head was in a whirl. Just as she had been wishing she could sever the tenuous ties that bound her to her husband, he desired to strengthen them. Why now, after seventeen years? He wished to make amends? How?

Stanton neatly carved a slice from the breast of a plump goose and placed it on his grandmother's plate. "May I carve some for you, Mamma?"

"If you please," she said absently. "You do that very well. I must speak to Cook about teaching Jasper."

He nodded as he deftly severed a leg for himself. "The important thing is to have the knife really sharp. A blunt blade is useless."

"I quite agree," Mr Harte said. "Make sure he is taught how to sharpen a knife properly as well, Duchess. You will want your own carving set at Oxford, Stanton, and never allow another to use them."

"No, sir. What else do you recommend I take with me? My father suggests a chafing dish."

Flora was happy to let the two converse across her, throwing in the odd word so that she still seemed to be part of the discussion. Opposite her, at the foot of the large table, her husband inclined his head towards his mother. He seemed his usual self while she was 'all of a dither', as Nurse used to say. How dared he upset her so and then behave as if nothing had happened?

With the second course, Lady Ottilia claimed Stanton's attention and Mr Harte turned to Flora. "We are looking forward to seeing my niece again at the May festivities. We had been afraid her new circumstances would prevent her from coming as usual."

"So was I. I am delighted Mr Fitzmaurice comes too. I hope the weather is more spring-like by then. Everything is very late this year."

"Better late than never," he said philosophically.

Was that how she should consider Gracechurch's apparent change of heart? It had not been easy for him to approach her. She should listen to him, at least, she supposed.

"May I help you to some trifle, Duchess?"

"Thank you."

Mr Harte set a sweetmeat glass in front of her.

"Trifle? Excellent." Stanton helped himself. His eyes widened as he tasted the layers of rich cream, silky custard and savoy biscuits spread with raspberry jam and soaked in brandy. "This is not a schoolroom trifle."

Flora smiled. "No. Cook made one for them too. Which do you prefer?"

"Frankly, I cannot say. It is also very good made with orange juice. I might drop by the kitchen later, see if they have left any—compare the two."

She might ask Cook to try using orange wine instead of brandy, Flora thought. She wondered if Olivia had made more this winter when the Seville oranges were in season. Perhaps she would part with her mother's recipe. She looked down the table. Everyone had finished eating. She caught her mother-in-law's eye and rose.

The gentlemen stood with the ladies. Stanton looked at his mother questioningly.

"Remain with the gentlemen," she murmured as she passed him and he nodded.

It was an hour before the gentlemen came up to the drawing-room. Flora looked carefully at her son. He was a little flushed but steady on his feet.

"We tarried too long, I am afraid," Gracechurch said, coming to sit beside her. "We were speaking of Oxford and Stanton was very interested in our stories."

"I can imagine," she said dryly.

He cocked an eyebrow at her. "Imagine what?"

"That your stories had very little to do with your studies. Earlier, Mr Harte took pains to impress upon him the desirability of having his own carving set."

He shrugged. "He will not always be at his books. Part of a university education is making new friends, getting to know your own generation. He will want to invite his friends to his rooms now and then."

"I suppose so, but Gracechurch, he is quite serious-minded, you know, and sincerely wishes to learn. I hope you will talk to him—I cannot advise him and I should like to encourage him. He is more interested in natural philosophy than ancient languages, he said."

"That is good to know. I shall make some enquiries when we are up, find out whom he should talk to."

She dropped her voice. "Thank you. He should enjoy himself as well, of course, but I do not wish to see him turn into an idle young man, interested only in the next spree. You know the sort—one encounters them every year, new on the town. Some settle down, but others become the worst sort of profligate. As heir to a great position, Stanton will be the target of every Captain Sharp, not to mention the toadies and leeches. It is good that you have started to take an interest in him—you will be better able to guide him than I."

"I should have done it before, not left it all to you," he returned, then sat back as the tea-tray was brought to her.

Flora busied herself making the tea. She looked at her son. Was he sober enough to hand the teacups? There was only one way to find out and better fail the attempt here than in some fashionable matron's drawing-room. He managed the little task successfully and returned to sit beside Mr Shorland. They were still discussing Oxford. Of course, Shorland was the nearest in age to him; the most recent student. Lady Ottilia and Mr Harte were ensconced on one sofa and Gracechurch remained beside her.

"I must tell you that the vicar always dines here on Easter Day."

He shrugged. "He is a pleasant enough fellow—Miss Humphreys' brother, is he not?"

"Yes. It's just—he is always happy to dine with us in the old house, but I cannot expect him to sit with the children if I am not there."

He raised that eyebrow again. "You do not propose to remain with them, I trust?"

"Yes and no. We shall dine early, at five o'clock, and the children will join us."

She had decided this after he announced his intention of coming to Stanton for Easter. Usually Miss Humphreys remained with the schoolroom party when Gracechurch was in residence, but Flora would not ask her to do so while her brother sat at the ducal table.

"That is an excellent solution," Gracechurch commented.

Lady Ottilia put down her tea-cup and rose stiffly to her feet. She kissed Flora and Stanton. "This has been a delightful evening, my dear. You have grown into a fine young man, Stanton. You must come and see me before you leave for Oxford."

"Certainly, Grandmamma."

"You may give me your arm down those interminable stairs, Gracechurch. I wish someone could invent a way of wafting us from one floor to another."

Flora watched them leave, accompanied by Mr Harte. Gracechurch's secretary bowed. He always withdrew once tea had been taken. "I beg you will excuse me, Duchess."

"Of course, Mr Shorland."

"I'll say goodnight too, Mamma."

She stood on tip-toe to kiss Stanton's cheek. "Good night, my love. Remember, church in the morning."

When the door closed behind the two men, Flora remained standing, staring at nothing. How was she to deal with this changed husband? Was he sincere? Would the change last? She had never refused him her bed unless she was indisposed but suddenly she felt she could not bear it if he came to her tonight. It would be too—personal.

She shivered suddenly. The fire had died down. Should she ring for a footman to replenish it or should she retire? She went to the window. Below, the golden lights from the twin carriage-lanterns bobbed down the avenue. Would Gracechurch return to the drawing-room? Did it matter if he found it empty? She shook her head impatiently. She had never cared about these things before. Why should she start now? She headed purposefully for the door, only to walk into her husband who caught her by the shoulders.

"Oh! I beg your pardon—my head was in the clouds. Gracechurch, your hands are icy!"

He released his steadying clasp at once. "Are they? I am sorry—it has turned devilish cold."

"I was just about to retire."

"Without a light? Although I suppose I should count myself lucky you were not carrying one." He stepped past her and picked up a silver candlestick. "I shall be your linkboy."

She allowed him to light her across the landing and down the shadowy passage to the big mahogany doors that guarded their private apartments. When they entered the central saloon, he lit more candles. She picked one up.

"I'll bid you goodnight, Gracechurch. If you wish to accompany us to church, we leave at a quarter to eleven."

He met her eyes and bowed slightly. "Very well. Goodnight, Flora." There was her name, again. Then, before she knew what was happening, he had bent and kissed her cheek. "Sleep well, my dear." He opened the door to her bedchamber and stood back to let her pass but did not attempt to follow.

Her hand was shaking and she hastily set down the candlestick. Tears pricked at the back of her eyes. It was almost twenty years since someone kissed her goodnight. Oh—she had dispensed thousands of goodnight kisses, but somehow this was different.

Chapter Eight

Easter Sunday had been enlivened by an unseasonal snowfall and an impromptu snowball fight on the way home from church. "I usually eat lunch with the children at half-past one o'clock," Flora said as they mounted the Priory stairs. "Do you care to join us? I should warn you that today the language of the table is French."

"*Quelle bonne idée*," Gracechurch said blandly. "*Je serai enchanté.*"

To his mild amazement, he very much enjoyed his *déjeuner à la fourchette*. Even Tabitha was reasonably fluent and both Flora and Miss Humphreys had the knack of supplying a missing word or making a gentle correction without interrupting the flow of conversation. They spoke French three times a week, he discovered.

"You do not serve French food," he remarked as he helped himself to a dish of eggs.

"I think it too rich for the children," Flora answered.

"How is it different?" Jasper wanted to know.

"It is more fancily dressed, with different sauces. We prefer our roasts, but they love their *ragouts*."

"We should try it," Tabitha said instantly. "I am nine now—that is old enough. After all, French children must eat French food, must they not?"

"I imagine so," Flora said. "I shall ask Podmore to speak to Cook and enquire what might be suitable for children. In the meantime, finish your English bread and butter. You must rest this afternoon if you are to dine with us later."

"*Oui,* Mamma."

"I confess I should not mind varying the schoolroom food," Flora said to her husband later. "And, now that I come to think of it, if they are not given a taste for more elaborate dishes, they may never come to like them. Perhaps that is why one gets such a poor dinner in so many houses."

"That's very likely. But it sounds as if you always eat with the children."

"And Miss Humphreys. If I do not have guests or dine out, I do. It rarely happens in town, of course, but we dine together most days here. I prefer it to sitting in state on my own. What do you generally do?"

"I seldom eat at home," he admitted. "If I am not engaged elsewhere, I'll have something at Whites."

"Do you never entertain?"

"Rarely." He smiled ruefully. "I pay my debts in that respect when you come to town. I enjoyed our lunch today. May I come again tomorrow?"

"If you wish."

"I should like to. We shall see this evening how the children take to richer fare."

If the younger children were initially subdued by the prospect of dining formally with the adults, they nonetheless contrived to make a good meal. To Gracechurch's amusement Tabitha, who sat on his right was the more adventurous of the two, insisting on being served from every dish she could see, even the oyster patties whose crisp, golden pastry crust proved too tempting.

He cut off the corner of one and put it on her plate. "Try this first. Oysters have a unique flavour, you will find."

She obediently popped the morsel into her mouth. He had to struggle to keep a straight face as her expression changed to one of appalled revulsion. She stopped eating and looked frantically from side to side as if there was some way she could dispose politely of the titbit.

"Swallow it down quickly, as if it were a paregoric draught," he recommended, adding, "Some orgeat for Lady Tabitha," to the butler who stood behind his chair.

Gracechurch handed the glass to his daughter. "Now drink this."

Her face cleared as she sipped the milky-looking liquid. "This is delicious. Thank you, sir. It has quite taken away the terrible taste."

Jasper, meanwhile, devoted himself to a leg of chicken and some slices of ham, but was induced to try the asparagus by the prospect of using his fingers instead of a knife and fork. The appearance of a dish of apple puffs together with some glasses of orange jelly in the second course proved a great success and Flora had wisely refrained from ordering a further course. She withdrew with the ladies and children, the gentlemen following them to the drawing-room some twenty minutes later.

As soon as the vicar took his leave, Miss Humphreys and the children returned to the old house. Stanton went with them, good-naturedly promising another game of Fox and Geese, this time pitting his and Tabitha's geese against Jasper's fox.

Flora dropped onto the sofa. "My mind's abuzz with rhymes and riddles."

Gracechurch smiled at her. "They are very quick, especially the boys. I felt quite mutton-headed beside them."

"Riddles and conundrums are all the rage among schoolboys. Jasper gets them from John Rembleton. Olivia sends them as a post-script to her letters."

"Does Jasper return the favour?"

"Yes. Stanton keeps him supplied with new ones."

Gracechurch shook his head at the idea of a flourishing correspondence in schoolboy riddles. "A glass of Madeira?"

"No, thank you. Pour me some cherry cordial, if you please."

He handed her a glass filled with dark ruby liquid and sat beside her. "May we talk now?"

And with that, Flora vanished. In her place sat the Duchess of Gracechurch. In not much more than twenty-four hours he had learnt to distinguish between the two. The duchess angled her body into the corner of the sofa and stretched her legs so that he had to retreat to give her room. She regarded him with an air of cool composure, the glass she held between her finger-tips a delicate barricade.

"Flora."

Her chin came up and she looked away, as if to reprove him for using her name. He cleared his throat. What was he to say to her?

"Flora, I beg you to listen to me. We shall soon be eighteen years married, we have three children and we might as well be strangers. It is not your fault," he added hastily, "it is mine. I am well aware that I kept you at a distance from the beginning. Now, I want to try and make amends; become better acquainted with you and the children."

She raised her eyebrows. "Why this sudden change of heart?"

The answer came unbidden and was spoken before he had time to reflect. "Because I realised that mine is a hollow heart and my life a hollow one. I have become an automaton; I discharge my duties but I exist rather than live. Nobody cares if I live or die."

"Your mother would care; so would I."

His heart leapt at her quiet words but he could not believe them. "Would you really? And would it be out of duty or affection?" When she flushed, he went on recklessly, "Flora, can you honestly say that in your heart of hearts you would not be grateful to be rid of me, free of your—our—marriage?"

She met his eyes. "No, I cannot say that—but not if my freedom comes about through death or—disgrace."

"Disgrace?"

"Divorce. It would mean disgrace, for me at least. Unfortunately, we cannot simply agree to part. I cannot divorce you; you would have to repudiate me for immoral behaviour and drag me through the courts. I would be ruined."

"You have clearly thought about this."

A little smile touched her lips. "Frequently. What, did you think the realities of our present situation had escaped me?"

"You never said anything."

She shrugged. "It would have been pointless. It is too late to claim an annulment on the grounds that I was coerced into marrying you; besides, it would probably bastardise the children and I would not want that."

She spoke so matter-of-factly, as if her deliberations were long in the past. It had never occurred to him that she might want to leave him. He had not expected her to welcome him with open arms, precisely, but he had assumed that she would be willing to let him try to bridge the ravine that lay between them. Now it appeared she preferred to turn away, to escape completely. "But if you could, you would divorce me?"

"If we could make a clean, amicable break with proper provision for me and no repercussions either for me or the children, yes. But it is impossible, I know. I would be banished from good society, no longer received at court— unable to present Tabitha, for example. But I do not wish you dead."

"Why not?" he asked bitterly. "As dowager duchess you would retain your high rank. Or you could marry again, as my mother did."

She set down her untasted glass. "Why not? For two reasons—no, three. First, I could not wish any man dead, let alone the father of my children. Then, I do not want them to be orphaned—an indifferent father is better than none—and, indeed, I welcome the fact that you propose to take more of an interest in them. And, finally, I do not wish Stanton to inherit the burden of the dukedom too soon."

Well, he had asked for it, but her reasoning still stung. "You are glad that I propose to take more of an interest in the children," he repeated carefully. "I should like to become better acquainted with you as well. Can we not at least strive to be friends?"

"Friends!" She jumped to her feet. "Damn you, Gracechurch! What right do you have to ask that of me?" The words spilled from her, quicker and quicker. "Do you think you can simply return from wherever you have been all these years and decree that from now on all will be different? Why should I open my heart and my mind to you when all you have ever wanted from me is the occasional use of my body? And my fortune, of course."

"Flora!"

She rounded on him. "Do not call me that. You do not have the right to use my name. That privilege is reserved to my friends."

"What should I call you?"

"Duchess has served you perfectly well so far."

"Duchess, then."

She inhaled deeply and swallowed, then took another breath and another, struggling for composure. The hectic flush in her cheeks ebbed and the fire in her eyes died. She braced herself with both hands on the table where they had sat earlier playing games, where for the first time he had felt part of a family.

"I beg your pardon."

Her bleak tone was like a knife to his heart. "No," he said slowly, "I must seek yours. As usual, I have thought only of myself. I am not used to putting myself in another's place. You are right; you owe me nothing. The debt is all on my side."

He picked up a sheet of paper that had been neatly pleated into a dozen folds, each one scribbled upon, and flicked it open. "Consequences—one thing leads to another, like a flight of stairs descended all too easily. I let myself be persuaded to marry you. That was bad, but worse, I believed my father when he said I need not alter my way of life. Once I set foot on the primrose path—"

"Where did it lead you, your primrose path?"

He sat down heavily. "Eventually? To hell."

"To hell? What do you mean? Were you a gamester?"

Why not tell her? Get the whole thing into the open. He had nothing more to lose. "No, not that. I had a mistress—that will not surprise you, I think?"

"No." She drew out a chair and perched sideways on it, as if ready to depart at any moment.

"That was what my father meant—that I need not give her up. She was the young widow of a country innkeeper. That is how I met her—I sought refuge there from a storm not long after I came down from Oxford. When she came to me, she sold the inn and I bought a house in Surrey. She was not a high-flyer like Harriet Wilson, just a country-woman, simple and loving."

"I see."

What else was there to say? "We were two children playing house until—" He felt his throat constrict.

"Until?"

"She got with child."

His wife looked up at that. "You have another child, other children?"

He shook his head. "Had. A daughter—she only lived three hours. It was not long before Stanton was born. Meg was very ill afterwards. It was a very long labour."

She nodded slowly. "Did you leave her to come here for the christening?"

"Yes."

"How you must have resented us—Rowland and me."

"No, not that—but I could not rejoice properly either. Everyone lined up to congratulate me, but when I saw him in his christening robes, all I could think of was Annie in the little gown Meg had made for her. We had time to have her baptised, thank God. I don't think Meg could have borne it if she could not have been buried in hallowed ground."

Flora's eyes changed as if she, too were looking back into the past. "You were so distant then—and yet, you brought me that necklace. Out of duty, I suppose. I never wore it afterwards."

"I'm sorry," he said helplessly.

"Were there other children?"

"No. The midwife said something had been damaged when Annie was born. And Meg—she lies with her daughter these past eight years."

"Afterwards. Did you replace her?"

"No." He shifted uneasily. It had never occurred to him to set up another mistress. His infrequent comings together with his wife had sufficed. He had remained faithful, he supposed, but to whom—his wife or to Meg's memory?

"Do you still mourn her?"

"I don't know. She—they belong to another life, another world. There was no-one I could tell. But I couldn't forget them either. Sometimes I think I am a castaway, stranded in some arid limbo between there and here."

He stretched his hand towards her. "Don't dismiss me, Duchess. Please." To his horror, his voice cracked, silencing him.

Flora had never thought she would feel sorry for her husband, but he looked so desolate and—defenceless. What a strange word to associate with him. He had opened his heart to her, revealed its deepest wounds. To be expected to rejoice at the birth of his heir, with his daughter dead in her mother's arms. It was not to be borne. He had been only twenty-three. She wished she could whirl back in time and confront those two selfish men, his father and her grandfather, who had cared nothing for the happiness of their children.

His hand lay open on the polished table—hers to take or reject. And yet—dare she risk her hard-won contentment, even her heart? She could not wish anyone dead, she had told him. To ignore his whispered plea would be to condemn him to a living death.

What was harder—to forgive or seek forgiveness? If she considered herself a Christian, she must try. She slid her hand across the table. When it touched his, he took it gently, cradling it in both of his. This time when he kissed her hand, she did not pull away.

After some time he released her. Sitting back, he offered her a tentative, damp-eyed smile. "I don't know whether to apologise or thank you. Both, I think. I feel re-born."

She was as shaken. What had just happened? What would happen next? The Duchess had been stripped from her and she felt seventeen again. He seemed the same, glancing at her and looking away, as if unsure what to do next. She shivered.

He picked up her discarded shawl and draped it around her. "You are cold. I do not know why ladies feel it imperative to bare their necks and shoulders no matter how chilly it is."

"The same way gentlemen remain cocooned in superfine and swathed in starched muslin on the hottest of summer days."

"Then you have the advantage of us, I admit." He stirred the smouldering embers and added more logs to be caught by the new flames. "That's better." He gestured to the sofa. "Come, Duchess, let us not fall at the final fence."

He was right. If they drew back now, they may never again speak so frankly. "Yesterday, you said you had had a sudden insight. What was it?"

"I ran into Malvin—to be precise, he ran into me, coming out of Whites. Nearly knocked me over."

She listened while he told her of his discussion with Lord Malvin and later of the dinner at Malvin House. "My eyes were opened to a whole new world. It was as if they were connected by invisible strands of love, love that survived death. You could hear it in the way they spoke of Captain Malvin, for example. I envied them, even him, for having had that."

"You have no brothers or sisters, of course."

"No. I grew up surrounded by servants, nurses and tutors of every description, but generally alone. When I went to school, I had no notion how to deal with the other boys."

"Was it easier at Oxford?"

"A little. I made some friends but we lost touch."

"You were leading a very different life. They were young men on the town, carefree, while you had a mistress and later a wife and child, not to mention the responsibilities of the duchy at an early age."

"You are very kind, Duchess."

"I am trying to picture Stanton in just such circumstances. You were very young."

"You were even younger when we married. I never wondered what it was like for you. I could still have done the gentlemanly thing. Meg wanted me to—she said it wasn't right that I continued to come to her after we were married. She tried to turn me away, but I wouldn't go, and in the end, she could not deny me. You did not care whether I came or went. I don't blame you—why should you? I was caught in a trap of my own making. Now, I regret what I did to both of you—poor Meg always felt a little guilty and you—if not for me, you might have married a man who would have been a better husband to you."

"My grandfather was determined to make a splendid match for me before he died—there were other peers who would have made much worse husbands—degenerate debauchees. I didn't understand that at the time, but your mother did."

"Perhaps our marriage saved you from that, at least. If so, I am glad. Duchess, do you think we might go back and start again?"

"Where would we start?"

"Perhaps by putting aside the Duke and Duchess. You are Flora and I am—" he faltered, uncertain what name to claim.

"You are?"

"Jeffrey George Rowland, but only my mother ever called me Jeffrey, and that rarely. To everyone else I was

Baldock, as Stanton was before I came into the title—or 'my lord', of course."

"I wonder did it affect your—your sense of self to be known by a title rather than a name," she said thoughtfully, "especially when your title changed three times. And with the final change, you became your father, one might say."

He made a face. "I suppose one might."

"How did Meg address you?"

"I told her I was James Charles. If she used my name, she tended to say Mr Charles."

"Hmm. We cannot have two Rowlands. Jeffrey or George then? Which do you prefer?"

"George is not a name I have ever associated with myself."

"I suppose not, especially as the FitzCharles are descended from the Stuarts. We must not forget your disreputable royal ancestor. I wonder why your father included George."

"He was anxious to demonstrate his loyalty to the Hanoverians, I think. Don't forget his mother was said to be a Jacobite. I have always suspected that some of my grandfather's debts may be traced to the forty-five."

"Aha. That may explain why my grandfather came to your father's assistance after your grandfather's death. My family always supported the Stuarts. I often thought it was one of the reasons he proposed our match."

"Better a Stuart on the wrong side of the blanket than none at all?"

"Precisely. By what name do you think of yourself?"

"Gracechurch, I suppose. It is the name I have borne longest. And you?"

"Flora." She paused and then said, "How have you thought of me up to now?"

He was silent for some minutes. At last he said, "As my wife."

"A possession?"

"No! Never that."

"An encumbrance, then?"

Another silence. Finally, he took a deep breath. "If I am to be frank, in the beginning, yes. Then, after my father died, a support, a bulwark even. You became the perfect duchess—accomplished, beautiful, irreproachable in all things—"

"Not only fertile but son-bearing," she concluded dryly. "Apart from that, I might as well be a marble statue—non-demanding, non-thinking, non-feeling—"

"But you are not, are you?" he interrupted. "Now I must learn who you are, who Flora is."

"You must also discover who Jeffrey is."

"Will you help me?"

"Yes, just—not tonight," she said wearily, "not tonight."

Chapter Nine

Despite her exhaustion, Flora was unable to sleep. Her husband's astonishing confession occupied her mind, sending her restless thoughts scurrying from one revelation to another. Jeffrey, he wanted her to call him now. His mistress had addressed him as Mr Charles. Many married couples used such a formal address. Presumably the woman had thought it more respectable to maintain the appearance of matrimony. Or perhaps this Meg had preferred to use endearments. Better not ask. He had been surprisingly frank, but there were some things Flora did not want to know.

All those years ago, when her grandfather told her of the match he had made for her, she had been both nervous and excited. The sixteen-year-old Flora would have tumbled head-over-heels in love with her handsome bridegroom had he made the slightest effort to woo her. Looking back, perhaps she should be grateful that he had not. She could not accuse him of direct unkindness either, but neither had he been particularly kind. His sins were more of omission than commission.

They had been married by special license in the saloon of her grandfather's house—the old man had made his painful way in from his bedchamber to give her away and the witnesses were the duke and duchess and Miss Humphreys.

Her husband had come to her that night and following their prosaic coupling, the party left for London the next day, she and the duchess sharing the carriage while the duke and his heir rode beside it.

When she went to say goodbye to her grandfather, he framed her face in his hands and kissed her brow. "You will be well looked-after now, child, and later one of the highest ladies in the land. Farewell until we meet in Heaven."

As there had been no time to order bride-clothes beforehand, they were to spend the first weeks of their marriage in town in the apartments reserved at Gracechurch house for the heir and his wife. This was also, as Flora later realised, to give her husband the opportunity to get her with child. Long sessions with the fashionable mantua-makers were followed by interminable hours pent up in the small drawing-room, unable to move or speak, while Mr Lawrence painted the double portrait that still hung there, but even this mutual discomfort had not served to ease the constraint between the newly-weds. Flora felt tongue-tied in her husband's presence, and despite all Miss Humphreys' instruction on the importance of maintaining an easy flow of conversation in company, could never think of a topic that might interest him. She was too dull for him, she concluded, as having once again assured himself that he found her well, he immersed himself in the latest issue of the Gentleman's Magazine.

He came to her bed regularly those first months but as soon as she announced her pregnancy, preparations were made for her to remove to Stanton to await the birth of their child. Her mother-in-law had hinted that all would be different once a new heir was born, and suggested she use the intervening months to prepare herself for her new position. The death of her grandfather within a month of their marriage provided a convenient pretext for her not yet going into society. Now an exclusive finishing governess was employed to instill the qualities required in a future duchess, while a French maid in collaboration with the foremost modistes and milliners ensured that her wardrobe had just that certain something that distinguished her from the rest.

It fell to her mother-in-law to inform her son of the birth of his child and some days later Flora received a little note saying that he was relieved to hear that she had been safely delivered and that she and the infant were well. He would come to Stanton at his earliest convenience, he wrote. This, it emerged, was to attend the christening some eight weeks later. By then, she had recovered from the agony and euphoria of giving birth. She had flatly refused to entertain the idea of a wet nurse. Feeding her son gave her a new purpose and she delighted in the small changes she observed in the infant day by day, in the first smiles and incoherent sounds that, she knew, were meant for her. At last there was someone to welcome and return her love.

Poor Jeffrey, she thought. She had a sudden image of him standing frozen-faced in her bedchamber, looking down at the child and then, very slowly, touching a finger to its cheek. He must have been close to shattering. Supposing he had broken down, fallen to his knees before her and confessed all? How would she have responded? Would she have had the compassion and generosity to forgive him? Probably not, she admitted to the silent darkness.

Unable to bear it any longer, she slipped from her high, curtained bed and made her way across the room to the hearth. She felt for a spill and touched it to the glowing embers, then carefully guarded the little flame until a pair of candles burnt brightly in front of the mantelpiece mirror. A warm shawl was folded on a daybed. She huddled into it, dropped into a low chair beside the dying fire, and drew up her feet under the hem of her night-gown.

Tears pricked her eyes. She wanted to cry, cry for them all caught in that merciless tangle so long ago, cry for poor, dead Meg and her baby, for Jeffrey, and for herself. She had schooled herself not to hanker after what she could not have, to eradicate the longing for love from her heart, retreating behind the public face that had long since become part of her. It had protected her against the wiles of the rakes of the *ton* and helped her resist the rare suitor who could have tempted her into more than a flirtation. Such dalliances, the sensible duchess had observed, exacted too high a price for a temporary pleasure. Instead, she gathered about her a circle of young wives with distant husbands. Flora's Fillies, as they were known, were happy to offer each other mutual support and friendship. But was it enough?

She would be thirty-five this year—only half-way to her three-score and ten. Half of her life still to come. Dare she rip open old wounds and see if they would heal without scarring or would she risk too much? She had agreed 'to start again'. But how?

"From her Grace, your Grace. Her maid is waiting for a reply."

Gracechurch unfolded the little note.

J.

The tailor calls this morning to measure Stanton for a new wardrobe for Oxford. I should be obliged if you would make Grimes available to advise him.

F

"Say I'll be with her Grace in twenty minutes if that is convenient for her."

Gracechurch sat impatiently while his valet finished shaving him. He dressed quickly in his usual country wear of pale buckskins, cream waistcoat and dark brown riding coat, his immaculate neckcloth tied in a deceptively simple knot. Slippers would do for now, he decided as he put on his seal ring. It was only ten o'clock. Flora was very likely still in her bedchamber. He would try there first.

To his surprise, she stood at the window of the saloon that formed the centre of their private apartments. It always struck him as a sort of sparsely furnished no-man's-land that served merely to separate their respective bedchambers, but seeing her waiting there made him say, "Could we do something with this room, make it more comfortable?"

She raised her brows. "I doubt it—with all the doors opening from it, it is more a hall or lobby than a sitting-room. The proportions are wrong too—it is too high for its width."

He looked around, dejected. "I suppose you are right. I just thought if we could make it more personal, snug and cosy, the way the Great Hall is now, we could spend time together here, get to know each other."

The words tumbled out of him. Was he making an almighty fool of himself? But Flora looked thoughtful.

"Have a neutral ground, you mean, or create a new territory?"

"Yes, one that is ours, not yours or mine. Do you like to play chess, picquet or anything of that nature? We could put in a games table and a bookcase, share our favourite books. I know it will take some time to have new furniture delivered, but I could have them bring up the games table and chairs from the library today."

"No, not today—in fact not before Stanton leaves for Oxford. I do not wish to cut short these last evenings I shall have with him."

"But you are not opposed to my suggestion?"

"Opposed in principle? No."

With that, he had to be content. "When is this tailor coming?"

"Coleston? In about half an hour."

"I've never heard of him. Does he come from town?"

"Yes. I requested Olivia to ask Mr Fitzmaurice to recommend a tailor who would know what younger men were wearing without insisting on providing every latest fancy. This man served his time with Weston who speaks highly of him, I understand. He will be more than happy at the prospect of having first crack of the whip at your heir. But I should like to have Grimes there as well. Stanton is a young man now—too old to have his mother select his wardrobe for him but he has not yet had to deal with a tradesman on his own. He will in Oxford, of course, but Grimes can give him a hint as to how to go about it."

How wise she was, willing to cede her maternal dominion without a battle—and that reminded him—he must make sure the boy had a decent allowance. But why would she seek the services of his valet when he himself was available? Because she was not sure he would agree, he thought dismally. Aloud, he said, "I'll speak to Grimes, but I'll look in on this Coleston myself—see what he has to offer."

"Thank you. Now I must speak to Podmore about the preparations for May Eve."

Two days later, Gracechurch quartered his vast bedchamber like a hound in search of an elusive quarry. He felt more and more accepted by his children but how the devil was he to woo his wife? During the day she seemed always to be occupied—and he could not completely neglect his own duties—their evenings were spent *en famille* and each night she firmly bade him goodnight at her bedroom door. Did she imagine he was going to fall on her there and then or march her willy-nilly to bed? Truth be told, everything in him revolted against the idea of their usual prosaic coupling. He would not go to her until he could be sure that Flora, not the duchess, would welcome him.

But how to get her on her own? He must consider his approach. There was no point crashing through the undergrowth, she would only retreat further from him. He must lure her out from her covert, entice her to somewhere she would feel less vulnerable so they could talk undisturbed. But how? *The wise hunter seeking prey goes silently and stealthily*; whistling the bravura horn accompaniment to Caesar's aria, he began to plot.

A pale pink tulip lay on Flora's breakfast tray, a rolled paper tied to its stem.

"From his Grace, your Grace," her maid said, unable to conceal her curiosity.

"Thank you, Merle. That will be all."

Flora did her best to ignore the little missive, directing all her attention to her first cup of chocolate and a roll spread with butter and honey, but the roll was too sweet and the chocolate too hot. It would be a pity to let the flower wilt, she told herself, as she drew it from the restraining ribbon. The stem was too long for her little vase and she trimmed it with her embroidery scissors before filling the vase with water from the washstand ewer. She carefully dried the blades of the scissors before returning to her breakfast, taking the vase with her. Had Gracechurch sent to the greenhouses for the flower, she wondered? He had probably then handed the billet-doux to his valet to give to Merle. Such a unique occurrence would not go uncommented. He might as well have posted it in *The Gazette*.

Her hands trembled as she unrolled the sheet of paper.

My dearest Duchess,

She closed her eyes for a moment and then read on.

Today dawned bright and sunny and I write to invite you to drive or ride out with me. Apart from the pleasure of your company, I should value your insight on certain matters to do with Hawkins's proposed programme of works for the coming months.

I hope your arrangements for the day permit your accompanying me. If so, pray advise me of the time that is most convenient for you so that I can send the necessary instructions to the stables. Given your dislike of high-perch phaetons, I will not offer to drive you in mine; we can ride or take the gig. The choice is yours.

In anticipation of your command, my dearest Duchess, I remain your obedient husband and servant,
Jeffrey G

It was indeed a glorious day, too beautiful to remain indoors but—she reread the letter. It was flirtatious, familiar and too confident of a favourable response. A husband could not be accused of presumption as a suitor might, but—an instinct long dormant stirred deep within her. He should not have it all his own way. She tugged the bell-pull before going to her writing table.

When Merle hurried in, she handed her a note. "Take that to Lord Stanton and wait for an answer."

Fifteen minutes later, the maid returned. "His lordship will be pleased to join you, your Grace."

"Excellent. My compliments to his Grace and I shall be happy to ride with him at half-past ten o'clock. Lord Stanton will accompany us."

"Very good, your Grace. Which habit should I put out?"

"The new one."

Gracechurch tapped his riding crop idly against his boot as he waited in the hall for his wife. At least she was willing to engage with him, even if she had recruited Stanton as a sort of duenna. He did not doubt that he could contrive to dispense with his son at some stage during the morning. No lad of his age would be able to resist galloping ahead when the opportunity presented itself.

He turned at the sound of quick footsteps on the landing and stopped, transfixed. In place of the more usual masculine or military styled habit, Flora wore a light-blue gown cut high to the neck where it was trimmed with a delicate lace ruff. He could not see any fastenings; the gown fell smoothly to her feet, the fabric caressing her bosom like a lover while the folds of her caught-up train attracted the eye to the beautiful curve of her waist and hip, and a pretty foot shod in a blue half-boot. The neat brim of her matching hat framed her face without hiding it. Releasing his breath, he went forward to the foot of the stairs.

"Good morning, my dear. Is this the latest style of habit? It is most becoming."

"Thank you, Gracechurch. Is Stanton not here yet?"

"He is outside with the horses."

"I should have known."

When he stood back to let her pass, he saw the garment was fastened at the back, the excess fabric gathered in a short frill that drew the eye to her sweetly rounded rump. Had she always dressed so alluringly? How could he not have noticed?

He waved her groom to the mare's head and stooped to assist his wife mount. She looked surprised but at once placed her hand on his shoulder and her foot in his cupped hand so he could boost her as she sprang to the saddle. Once seated, she deftly hooked her right knee over the pommel then felt with her left foot for the stirrup he held steady for her. Her train released, she arranged her skirts gracefully and took the reins from the groom. Gracechurch swung into his own saddle.

"Where first?" Flora asked.

"To the footbridge over the stream. The handrail is loose and some of the boards are rotten, Hawkins said."

"It's good to be on horseback again," Stanton said as they rode away from the bridge that, all were agreed, needed to be repaired.

"You will need a mount in Oxford—a good-tempered hack is best. A bit of blood will only get restive in livery." Gracechurch nodded at the black gelding his son rode. "Why don't you try his paces, see how he suits you?"

Stanton's face lit up. "I'll do that. Thank you, sir."

"Is a horse really necessary in Oxford?" Flora asked as Stanton cantered ahead.

"Yes. He won't be able to keep up with his friends otherwise. Even if he applies himself to his books, he will be at liberty for much of the day. It is not at all like school."

"I gather that," she said dryly. "But speaking of schools, I wanted to talk to you about the situation here."

"School? I was not aware there was one." Gracechurch slowed his mount to a walk. "Do you think we need one? There are those who consider it a mistake to educate the lower classes for fear of encouraging radicalism."

"What nonsense! Denying them even the slightest opportunity to improve their lot is far more likely to radicalise them. Even the rudiments of an education make such a difference. Once children can read and write, they have a better chance of getting a good place—and are less likely to be cheated at market or elsewhere."

Secretly delighted by her heated response, he held up his hand, second finger crossed over the index one. "Truce! Truce! I agree with you. Tell me about the situation here."

This earned him a reluctant smile. "Do you recall old Miss Fortescue, the sister of the previous rector, who lived in the cottage beside the church? She was happy to teach the children whose parents were willing to send them to her. Apart from reading and writing, she taught a little ciphering, the catechism and also showed the girls how to sew a fine seam. She didn't charge—she said she loved to have the little ones come to her—but she never wanted for newly-baked bread or fresh eggs or a bottle of cowslip wine.

"There can be no doubt that the regular association with a lady such as Miss Fortescue teaches children how to behave and inculcates them with a proper respect for their betters. Podmore has frequently remarked to me that she much prefers to take a village girl and train her up than employ a flighty town maid when she doesn't know where she comes from or who her people were."

"I see. Miss Fortescue is no longer with us, I take it."

"No. She died just before Christmas."

"I had not realised. Is there no-one who might take over from her?"

"No. But I think we need something more than a makeshift dame school. Mr Humphreys agrees and suggests we establish one under the auspices of the Society for Promoting Christian Knowledge, as he can be sure then that the children are instructed according to the teachings of the church."

"A Sunday school, then?"

"It need not be. In some places, the children are taught three days a week, the boys in the morning and the girls in the afternoon. Remember, most of them must work at home or on the land and their parents will not be able to spare them for more than that."

"In principle, I am not opposed to the idea," Gracechurch said thoughtfully, "but this would be a permanent commitment and we must consider if the estate should bear the full cost."

She nodded. "A school requires premises, a teacher or teachers and funds to support it but it need not all come from us. Miss Fortescue's cottage might be suitable for a schoolmaster, or if we found a suitable couple, a curate and his wife, provided he were willing to teach the boys and she the girls. In many places, the lessons are held in the church and we could do that in the beginning at least, until we see if there is the need for a proper schoolhouse."

"Was that also Humphreys' suggestion? A curate is generally paid from the tithes, which would reduce his income."

"If it is to be a dual role, all the expense should not fall to him. He is now more than sixty and finds winter more and more trying. He has been saying he should relinquish the living to a younger man but welcomed the idea of a curate as it would mean that he could remain here, near his sister." She hesitated for a moment. "Miss Fortescue's income came from an annuity that died with her, but she left everything she possessed to me, to dispose of at my sole discretion for the good of the parish."

"She did, did she? Do you get many such bequests?"

"No. That was the only one, thank Heaven. She did ask me first—she did not want to seem presumptuous—and I felt I could not refuse her."

"Why not? It was quite an imposition."

"There was no one else she could rely upon to be discreet, especially with her papers, and she no longer had the strength to do it herself. I took charge of them after she died and Podmore and I went through everything else. She had already made a suitable gift to Jane Smith, her maid, who cared for her most faithfully until the end. We consulted the churchwardens' wives as to who should have her clothes but everything else is still there—all her furniture and household goods including her and her brother's books. I thought the whole parish would benefit from a curate or schoolmaster and why dispose of items we might be grateful for later."

"That was wise."

"I was sorry for the old lady—she was so alone and completely dependent on strangers for the last services." She brushed her hand across her eyes and smiled mistily. "Though perhaps I need not have been. Every former pupil within five miles and many from further afield came to see her buried. So many plum cakes were handed in to the rectory for the funeral feast that I thought they would never all be eaten, but there was hardly a crumb left."

"That is a better ending to your story. Unlike Caesar, the good that she did lived after her."

"I like to think so. After everything was paid and money set aside for a tombstone, there are twenty-five pounds left which can be used to purchase slates and some primers for a school."

"Has the cottage been empty since Christmas?"

"No. I agreed with Hawkins that Jane could continue to live there until it was decided what to do with it, provided she looks after it properly. She is a good worker and I hope that a new tenant will keep her on."

He smiled at her. "I am ashamed to say I had not realised that you were so involved with the tenantry. You put me to shame."

She flushed. "Many ladies of quality do not concern themselves with such matters, I know, but they are all our people, are they not? This was an exceptional case, I admit; Miss Fortescue was a lady, and as the rector is a bachelor, she turned to me."

"We'll leave the horses at the *King's Arms*," Gracechurch decreed when they reached the village.

All work ceased as they clattered into the inn yard, grooms and postilions backing away, bowing deeply. A muttered command sent one lad darting indoors while the head groom came to stand beside Flora's horse. By the time two others waited by Gracechurch's and Stanton's mounts, the landlord and his wife had burst onto the scene, she still tying a clean apron behind her back.

"Your Graces, my Lord, what an honour. Do you care to dismount? How may we serve you?"

"For now, we propose to leave our horses here."

Gracechurch swung down from the saddle and went to assist his wife. She brought her leg lithely over the pommel and set her hands on his shoulders as he lifted her down. Her body was warm and supple and he held her close for a moment longer than necessary before setting her on her feet.

She murmured, "Thank you," then nodded civilly to the awestruck landlady and her husband. "Pray send somebody to the vicarage. My compliments to Mr Humphreys, and I should be obliged if he would join us at Miss Fortescue's cottage." She took a little coin-purse from her pocket and handed the landlady a shilling. "For the messenger," she added, then deftly gathered up her train, tucked her free hand into Gracechurch's arm and piloted him out of the yard. Stanton fell in on her other side.

"Why did you send for Mr Humphreys?" Stanton asked as they walked along the cobbled street to an accompaniment of bows, bobs and tugged forelocks. "Do we—you not have the disposal of the living?"

"Yes," Gracechurch answered, "but once an incumbent has taken possession of the parish, it is his until he chooses to vacate the living. The decision to take an assistant curate is also his, not mine."

"What if you wished to dismiss a rector?"

"I cannot do so at whim, or because I wish to offer the parish to another. It would have to be for a very good reason, and following due process. The bishop would have to be involved."

"So you may not deliver yourself of a turbulent priest?"

"It would depend on the nature of the turbulence," Gracechurch said with a grin. "Certainly nothing that Mr Humphreys could be accused of."

"What do you think makes a good schoolmaster, Stanton?" Flora asked.

The boy looked taken aback but then said, "It is easier to say what he shouldn't be."

"What is that?"

"Some masters are very hot-tempered and get up in the boughs if a fellow doesn't understand something at once. They think they can flog it into them, which of course they can't. It only makes matters worse. And some of them are better at explaining than others. And they shouldn't have favourites either or make fun of the weaker ones."

"So you would say the ability to convey knowledge and an amiable disposition are most important?"

"Yes. They must be firm, of course, and not shilly-shally or let pupils get away with too much. Fellows don't mind if a master is firm as long as he's fair."

"One would look for the same qualities in a curate," Gracechurch remarked.

"He must be intelligent and gentlemanly," Flora said, "perhaps a younger man who could later take over from Mr Humphreys. We'll see."

Chapter Ten

Flora glanced sideways at her husband as they left the village. This past couple of days he had revealed a surprising amiability of disposition, willingly acceding to any request, whether it was Tabitha's desire to demonstrate her new dancing steps or Jasper wishing to observe his father's fencing bouts with Stanton. Now Gracechurch had accepted her arguments in favour of founding a village school and spoken approvingly of her concern for the tenants.

"Where next?"

"I want to look at the west gate lodge," he answered. "It would be useful to have someone living there so that the gates are not always locked."

"The Bateson's youngest, Dan, is back at home. He gets quite blue-devilled, his mother told me, because he cannot work on the farm the way he did before, but he should be able to manage the gates quite easily. He has a pension of a shilling a day and if he could earn a little more as gatekeeper, he would do well enough, especially as he would have the lodge rent-free."

"Why can he not work on the farm?" Stanton asked.

"He lost his left leg below the knee at Waterloo. They have fitted him with a wooden one so he can get about but he is too unsteady in the fields." She broke off at the sight of a boy pelting towards the village, calling as he came abreast of them. "Tommy, what is wrong?"

The lad stopped, chest heaving, and used his sleeve to wipe the perspiration dripping into his eyes. "Please, yer Grace, it's my new Mam; I'm to fetch Mrs Godley as quick as possible, my Da says. The baby won't come—it's tearing her apart."

"Is your mam at home, Tommy?"

The boy nodded.

"We'll come at once," Flora said.

An indescribable sound, a combination between a grunt and a groan had her look at her husband. He had gone chalk-white.

"Mrs Godley lives about a mile away on the other side of the village," she said rapidly. "Stanton, take Tommy up before you and ride back with your father. Tommy will show you her cottage. I'll go ahead and see what I can do to help."

"But—"

She held up a hand to stop her husband's protest. "There is no time to argue. Go!" She tapped her heel and her switch against the mare's flanks, calling over her shoulder as she left, "He's Tommy Bolton, the gamekeeper's son."

And their cottage was at the edge of the woods, Flora thought grimly, with no immediate neighbours. Tommy must have been running for a good twenty minutes, judging by his state. His mother had died three years previously, and to everyone's surprise, Bolton had married the head dairy-maid a year later. This was their first child.

She turned into the lane that led to the gamekeeper's cottage. When she reached the house, she slid to the ground and led the mare to the yard at the back where she looped the reins around a post. "Good girl," she murmured, patting the horse's neck. "Stay here—I'll see if I can send someone to look after you."

With a quick prayer that at least she would do no harm, Flora opened the back door of the cottage. The kitchen was empty. Everything was spotless, as befitted a former dairymaid, but the fire had almost died down. She stripped off her gloves and dropped them and her switch on the table. A long, deep groan from above broke the hushed silence. She caught her skirts tightly about her and set foot on the narrow, steep stairs. "Mrs Bolton? Mrs Bolton? May I come up?"

Floor-boards creaked. A door was wrenched open and Bolton, dishevelled and barefoot, clad only in his shirt and breeches, peered down at her. His eyes widened. "Your Grace! What? I mean—"

Behind him, another long, low groan had him flinch and look over his shoulder. "Maisie."

"We met Tommy," Flora said as she rapidly mounted the stairs. "The duke rode back with him for the midwife and I came ahead. May I go in to your wife?"

"It ain't fitting, your Grace."

"Nonsense, man. Any woman must be happy to assist another in such straits, and Mrs Bolton was a member of my household for many years. Go down and make up the fire, and put some water on to heat, then watch for Mrs Godley. She cannot be long."

When she reached the small landing, he went back into the bedroom. "Maisie, here's her Grace come to see you."

"Her Grace!" The woman turned an appalled look on Flora as her husband slipped out of the room. She had collapsed against flattened pillows, her sweat-slickened dark hair sticking to her face. There was still a little water left in the heavy ewer. Flora dampened a cloth and gently wiped the woman's face.

Mrs Bolton sucked at the cloth with dry lips. "That's good—Ooooooooooooooooh—" She grabbed Flora's hand as the mound of her belly tightened and she began to bear down.

"How long has it been?" Flora asked when the spasm ended.

"Waters broke—last night—pains started—later."

It was now after one o'clock—she had probably been labouring for twelve hours.

"Lord Stanton took Tommy up on his horse and they rode back to the village for Mrs Godley," Flora said reassuringly. "They should be here soon."

"Tommy'll be that proud. He's a good—" Mrs Bolton broke off as another spasm gripped her.

Once it was over, Flora folded back the top sheet and blanket. "Mrs Bolton, pray forgive the liberty. Can you pull up your feet and plant them apart on the mattress?"

"Yes, 'm."

Flora tried frantically to remember what had happened during the births of her own children as she peered between the open thighs. "I can just see the head. You are doing splendidly."

The labouring woman tried to raise herself on her elbows. "If I could sit up a little, I could bear down better."

"Can you lean against me while I shake up your pillow and Bolton's as well?"

"I'll try—Oooooh."

"After this one." Flora slipped her arm under Mrs Bolton's shoulders, supporting her through the contraction. "Now."

Once her patient relaxed, Flora rapidly plumped up and turned the two goose feather pillows, set them against the wooden headboard and helped Mrs Bolton to slide up in the bed so that she could recline against the cool, smooth linen. The woman sighed with relief.

"That's better. Oh, thank you, ma'am," she panted as Flora gently passed the newly moistened cloth over her face and neck.

"Let's see how you go on," Flora said, going to the foot of the bed as the next contraction began. "I can see the crown. It won't be long now. Push as hard as you can, the next time, Maisie," she added, moving closer.

The sound of horses and voices outside was followed by a sharp rap on the front door.

"I must—" The woman on the bed strained and pushed.

"There's the head. Once more, now." Flora instinctively guided the tiny body as it slipped into the world. "A little girl," she said as a thin wail filled the air. "You have a daughter, Maisie."

"All done?" a voice said from the door.

"The baby is here, Mrs Godley, just this minute," Flora said. She had never been more relieved. "I'll leave you to look after her and Mrs Bolton." She handed the newborn to the midwife and went to the head of the bed. "Congratulations, Mrs Bolton."

"Thank you, your Grace and thank you for—" Mrs Bolton made an all-encompassing gesture. "I knew as soon as I saw you that all would be well. Will you tell Bolton?"

"Yes. I'll send him up with some warm water. Mrs Godley will make you more comfortable." She patted her former dairymaid's hand. "You did very well. I'll call again in a day or so to see how you go on."

They heard the faint wail of a newborn as soon as a wild-eyed Bolton opened the cottage door. The midwife pushed the gamekeeper out of the way and made for the stairs. Tommy ran to his father's side and Gracechurch and Stanton looked at one another, wondering what to do now. After a couple of moments, Bolton turned and stumbled into the kitchen where he collapsed onto a chair.

"Stanton and Tommy, take the horses and the gig around to the back," Gracechurch ordered as he followed the gamekeeper into the cottage.

The crying stopped and there was a babble of women's voices from upstairs.

"All seems to be well," Gracechurch said, taking a silver flask from his pocket. He took a glass from the dresser and poured a generous measure for his involuntary host. "Drink that," he commanded, before filling the cap of the flask for himself. His mind was too full of the last time he had ridden for a midwife. Mrs Godley's reassuring prattle had been all too familiar, but while his intellect informed him that most birthings ended happily, desolate memory persisted in reminding him that one could not count on it.

Bolton looked blindly at the glass, raised it to his lips and downed the contents in one. He shook himself like a wet dog. "Maisie?" he asked when he had caught his breath.

"Is doing splendidly," Flora said.

No-one had noticed her come downstairs. At the sound of her voice, the gamekeeper sprang to his feet and Stanton, who had come in the back door with Tommy, went to relieve her of the heavy ewer she carried.

"Your Grace?"

"Congratulations, Bolton. You have a beautiful daughter and mother and baby are well." She indicated the ewer. "Fill that with warm water and take it up to Mrs Godley."

He took the receptacle numbly from Stanton and went to the kettle that hung over the fire.

"Is there anyone to help while your wife is lying-in? Apart from Tommy, of course?" Flora added with a smile for the boy. "Any woman?"

"Maisie's mother is coming the day after tomorrow. We thought that would be time enough."

"Babies always think differently, you'll find. I'll send down one of the maids to help out until she comes."

"Thank you, your Grace." At the foot of the stairs, he turned and looked at his visitors. "I don't know what to say, your Graces, your lordship; 'thank you' don't seem enough."

"Don't worry about that," Gracechurch answered. "Go up to your wife and daughter."

As soon as Bolton was out of sight, Flora sank into his chair and put her head in her hands. She took a deep breath that was almost a sob.

"Flora?" Gracechurch knelt beside her and took her in his arms. "There now, all is well."

"Oh, Jeffrey!" Her hands and face were streaked with blood.

"See if there is any warm water left," he instructed Stanton, handing him his handkerchief, and turned back to his wife who clutched him as if she would never let go.

"I didn't know what to do—I could only be with her and, and catch the baby when it came."

"That was all that was necessary." He tenderly wiped her face and then gently released her hands, one by one, and cleaned them. She frowned, took the handkerchief from him, refolded it to a clean part and began to dab carefully at his coat.

"I was so thankful that Mrs Godley came—I didn't know how to cut the cord, or what to do about the afterbirth."

"You would have coped splendidly, I am sure of it."

She leaned her head on his shoulder. "I was so afraid, Jeffrey."

"But you did not let your fear stop you. That is real bravery." He smiled and touched the coquettish little feather in her hat. "Did you really deliver a baby wearing this? You must be the most modish midwife in the world."

She gave a watery chuckle and raised her head. "There wasn't time to take it off. I should have, I suppose. We should go—they'll do better without us."

He poured a tot of brandy into the cap of the flask. "Drink this first. Then we'll be off. "

She sipped obediently, made a face and sipped again, looking from him to Stanton. "You came back for me. That was good of you."

"I did not want you to have to face it on your own," Gracechurch said quietly. "If things had gone wrong—"

"But they didn't, thank God. And thanks to Tommy as well, who ran so fast." She looked at the boy. "Did you understand that you have a new little sister? You will be able to see her soon."

"She'll be very small," Stanton put in, "but she'll grow."

"Indeed." Gracechurch handed the boy a guinea. "For valour."

"Valour?" the lad stammered as he inspected the gold coin.

"Courage—giving all you have on the battlefield; the way you ran today. You did very well."

"Yes, indeed," Flora said. "Tommy, you should draw more water in case Mrs Godley wants some."

The task steadied the boy. He came out to the yard with them and waved as they rode away before picking up his bucket and going to the well.

The three rode back in silence. When they reached the priory, Stanton said, "Mamma, you go in directly. I'll see to your mount—yours too, sir, if you like."

"Thank you." Gracechurch dismounted, handed his son the reins then went to assist his wife.

"I'll have them serve lunch in the small dining parlour in half an hour, Rowland," Flora said to the boy. "It's quiet time in the schoolroom now."

"And woe betide us if we disturb it," he acknowledged with a grin as he led the three horses away.

"Quiet time?" Gracechurch asked as he and Flora climbed the stairs.

"The hour when Miss Humphreys rests. The children may occupy themselves as they wish as long as they are quiet. If they are not, they will find themselves with additional exercises to do after dinner."

She stopped at the door to her bedroom. "I shall see you again in half an hour, Jeffrey."

He bent and kissed her firmly. "For valour," he said when he raised his head. "Thank God you were with me, Flora."

Chapter Eleven

"**J**asper doesn't want to be with me anymore," Tabitha complained two days later. "He is either with Stanton or Stanton and his Grace. When he asks Miss Humphreys if he may go, she always says yes, but they never ask me and when I ask may I come too, Jasper says it is for boys and men, and not for little girls."

Flora looked enquiringly at Miss Humphreys.

"Lord Jasper likes to look on when his Grace and Lord Stanton practise with the foils, and accompany them when Lord Stanton has a driving lesson," the governess explained. "We must not forget that Lord Jasper goes to school in the autumn—I believe it is good for him to have as much masculine company as possible before then."

"It's boring without him," Tabitha said, "and when he goes to school, I shall be alone in the schoolroom. I wish I could go to school too."

"You are far too young for school," Flora said firmly, "and I am not sure that you would like it if you went. Most schools for young ladies are very strict, you know, and spend a lot of time learning by rote—Miss Mangnall's questions are very popular, I believe—but the important thing is to be able to rattle off the answer, not to understand it."

"Hmm."

"If you go to school you will not be able to come home for May Day. This will be Lord Jasper's last May Day until he comes down from Oxford," Miss Humphreys pointed out.

When her mother added, "Nor will he be able to come to town with us. This will be his last year," Tabitha burst into tears.

"But that will not be for years! I suppose John Rembleton will go to school as well, and it will only be Miranda and Samuel and me left. And Miranda and Samuel won't stay with us anymore—they will live in Mr Fitzmaurice's house. Nothing will be the same."

Flora took her sobbing daughter into her arms. "I know, but that does not mean that it will not be pleasant. We shall visit the Fitzmaurices, and they will visit us, I am sure. Why, they are coming here next week for May Day. Perhaps Mrs Fitzmaurice will permit her three to come and stay with us for a few days in London. And I am sure we will have our outing to Hampton Court as usual."

"Perhaps his Grace will come with us," Tabitha said. "We never have a gentleman of our own, and the Rembletons had first Mr Rembleton, then Captain Frobisher and now Mr Fitzmaurice. It's not fair."

"Perhaps he will. You could suggest it to him," Flora said, pricked by the note of jealousy in the girl's voice. "And I shall ask if he would like to ride with us tomorrow."

"Just you and me, not the boys?"

"If that is what you prefer."

"Yes. We can all go together another day," Tabitha said firmly. "We must make the most of the time his Grace is here. This is the longest I can remember him staying—I imagine he'll go back to town soon."

Would he, Flora wondered. He had only committed to remaining until May Day. What would happen then?

"There is a cold wind today. You will need a warm spencer over your habit," Flora warned her daughter the following day as Tabitha hurried away to get ready for their ride. "And don't forget your gloves."

"Perhaps we should postpone our expedition," Gracechurch suggested as the door closed behind their daughter.

"No, she is so looking forward to it. She is anxious to make the most of the time you are here," Flora added. "She assumes you will be returning to town soon."

Gracechurch didn't know what to say. He had found it easy enough to get onto good terms with his sons—males had enough in common, he supposed—but didn't know how to approach his daughter or what she expected of him.

Before he could ask his wife what she meant, she had dropped her napkin onto the table and stood. "I must change too. We shall meet you in the stable yard in twenty minutes."

He had his orders, Gracechurch thought, amused, as he went in search of a warmer coat and his riding gloves and whip.

Tabitha was already in the stable-yard when he arrived there, feeding chunks of carrot to a solid-looking bay pony as she crooned some nonsense to him. "And you must be on your best behaviour today because his Grace rides with us," she finished as Gracechurch came up to her.

"There you are, sir," she exclaimed. "Mama will not be long." She turned to the head groom who hovered nearby.

"Hope, may I give their Graces' horses some carrots too? I don't want them to feel left out."

"If you take it nice and steady, my lady, just the way I've shown you."

Gracechurch could not but be impressed by the sight of that small hand held fearlessly up to the equine mouths and was relieved to see Hope follow at the child's elbow, ready to intervene.

"So this is your pony," he said when she was finished.

"Yes, he is called Lightning for the zigzag blaze here on his forehead. Stanton named him. First he was Stanton's, then he was Jasper's and now he is mine. Maybe, when Jasper goes to Harrow, I can ride Marmaduke."

"You will have to grow some more before you will be big enough to ride Marmaduke," Flora said behind them.

She wore a wine-coloured habit with an ermine collar and had pulled a matching velvet toque trimmed with the same fur snuggly over her dark curls. She looked deliciously warm, Gracechurch thought as he went to help her mount. Hope tossed Tabitha, who had been hopping impatiently from one foot to the other, into the saddle and they were ready to depart.

"Where to?" Gracechurch asked.

"Just the round of the Park," Flora answered. "We can't dismount and leave the horses standing in this wind. Will you lead the way, Tabitha?"

The child rode well, Gracechurch thought, rising neatly to the trot and alert to anything untoward, as evidenced by her response when a wayward squirrel darted across the path almost under the pony's feet, causing it to shy and dance a little. Tabitha remained firmly in control, leaning forward a little to speak soothingly to her mount.

As soon as the danger was averted, he drew alongside her. "That was very well done."

She looked pleased at his compliment. "Thank you, sir. He was only a little startled, you know, and we are used to one another."

"I can see that. Will you be sorry when you grow too big for him?"

"A little. But we can keep him, can we not, to give rides to small children who visit us? He likes that."

"Does he?"

"Mmmm."

"What else do you like to do? You play the pianoforte, I know. Do you have other special lessons?"

"Dancing—I like that—and watercolours—I'm not as good at that as Jasper is."

"But Jasper is three years older."

She shook her head. "Even still. When I look at his paintings from when he was nine—they are much better than mine are now."

"There are some things you do better than Jasper, I imagine. Does he play the pianoforte, for example?"

"Yes, but he doesn't like it as much as I do. Miss Humphreys says it doesn't matter because he is a boy and won't be expected to play in the drawing-rooms as girls are."

Gracechurch laughed. "A gentleman who can play the piano and is willing to accompany a lady while she is singing is always at an advantage."

"Used you do that, sir?"

"A little. I preferred to play the flute but after I broke my wrist some years ago, I stopped."

Flora, who had come up on Tabitha's other side, looked curiously at him but said nothing. He had never played while she sang, he thought, or even sung with her. Something else to try.

"I can feel the first drops of rain," she said. "Should we turn into the avenue here rather continue our way around the Park."

"And canter?" Tabitha said hopefully.

"Why not."

They tacitly let the child set the pace, riding three abreast up the long avenue, slowing only when they reached the forecourt. Tabitha led them into the stable yard.

"That was famous," she gasped, cheeks glowing, as Gracechurch lifted her down onto the cobbles.

"Thank you for the invitation to join you," he said gravely. "I hope I may do so again."

"Oh, yes. Please, sir, if you would."

"I should be delighted to."

She nodded, suddenly shy, and ran to her mother but then looked back and said, "Thank you for coming with us, sir."

Smiling to himself, Gracechurch followed his ladies into the stair hall of the old house but when they continued up the stairs he went into the schoolroom. It was still quiet time. Stanton was ensconced by the fire reading while Jasper sat at a table on the gallery beside the big window. He had an easel in front of him and his brushes arrayed to one side. Curious, Gracechurch went up to look.

The boy was indeed talented, he thought, admiring the depiction of the ruined St Anthony's Priory beside the swiftly flowing stream. Storm-clouds were clearing, pierced by the shafts of sunlight dazzling in their intensity.

"You have portrayed the play of light exceedingly well," he commented.

Jasper grunted around the handle of the brush he held clamped between his teeth but continued what he was doing. After a couple of minutes he removed the brush, dipped it briefly into a clear yellow on his palette and carefully dabbed the colour on some tall, flat leaves growing on the river bank. Yellow flags, Gracechurch saw at once. It was not a botanical reproduction but the boy had somehow captured the essence of the flowers.

At last he rinsed his brushes and sat back. "I can do no more or it will all run together."

"It is very good," Gracechurch said.

Jasper shrugged. "It is hard to say. I have very little to compare it with. Most of the paintings here are in oil. There are some watercolours done by your great-aunts, I believe, sir, but they are very mannered."

"Have you been to the summer exhibition at the Academy?"

"No, sir."

"Would you like to go this year?"

"More than anything in the world!" Jasper cried. "Thank you, sir."

"I am not sure Harrow is the best place for Jasper," Gracechurch said that evening after Flora had left the gentlemen to their port. "What do you think, Stanton?"

"I had been wondering the same, sir," his son answered. "If you have an ear for the classics, a talent for sport and can stand your ground in a mill, you will do well enough but otherwise, it can be hard."

"And you don't think your brother would do well there?"

"Frankly, I doubt it, for the first couple of years at least. And by then the damage can be done."

"Is there much bullying?" Mr Shorland, who had been listening intently, asked.

Stanton shrugged. "There are always those who will pick on boys they perceive as weak or different—bullying, fagging, flogging—call it what you will. The hours outside lessons are devoted chiefly to sport. I enjoy cricket, football, rackets, bowls, but Jasper—well, he does not seem to have an eye for a ball. Some fellows do, it comes naturally to them, they will always catch it or hit it, but Jasper is not one of them so far as I can see. And if you do not have a taste for sport the days at school can be long and dreary." He looked at his father. "Dr Butler will want to have him in the Head Master's, I daresay, but in truth it is very over-crowded. Why, I've seen little boys eating their breakfast and supper in the yard, or even in the street. He would hardly have Jasper do that, of course, but it is not comfortable."

"What do you recommend, then?"

"He's very friendly with John Rembleton—perhaps he could go to Shrewsbury with him."

"It's a thought," Gracechurch answered. "Shall we join the duchess?"

"Not send Jasper to Harrow?" Flora said later to her husband. "I should be delighted to have him at home, of course, but I think he needs something more. Even Miss Humphreys thinks he needs more masculine companionship."

"We could consider engaging a younger man, one just down from Oxford, say, as tutor and companion for the summer and see how they go on together. He would come to town with us."

"That's a good idea. I'll talk to Olivia; see what plans she is making for John this year."

"I can take them about a little, to Tattersalls' for example, and I've promised Jasper to take him to the summer exhibition at the Academy. I hope you will come too, but I think Tabitha is still a little young for it, don't you?"

"Yes."

It felt very strange discussing the children with him the way she imagined normal parents would. If only she could be sure this change in him would last. They could not remain at Stanton forever—Tabitha was already looking forward to their usual sojourn in town. And he had promised to take Jasper to the Academy. She hoped he would remember. The children would be disappointed if his new interest in them faded once he returned to his usual haunts. But if it didn't?

"What are you smiling at?" he asked.

"I was picturing the bemusement among the *ton* at the sight of you accompanying us on our family outings. Tabitha has already expressed the hope that you will come with us on our annual excursion to Hampton Court. We take the shallop and it is always a very pleasant day."

His answering smile faded. "All those riches at my feet and I could not see to pick them up. Truly, there are none so blind as those who will not see. These last days have taught me so much. It has been a bitter lesson. When I think of the joyless life I have led in recent years, I am well-punished for my neglect of you."

"It will not help you now to dwell on it," she said gently. "You must continue to look forward, not back."

"You are right, I suppose." He took a breath. "As we are talking about education, while Miss Humphreys is an estimable woman, I wonder if she is not too old for Tabitha."

"Not yet, but almost. I have been thinking of making a change next year, once Tabitha is ten. I would prefer a younger governess, one who could be more of a companion for her and one who has more experience in preparing girls for their come-outs. While Miss Humphreys may know the theory, she does not know the practice. Ideally I should like to find a lady who has been with a *ton* family for some years, but a reputable *ton* family, of course, not one of the more dissolute ones."

He laughed. "I agree with you, but I also look forward to seeing you couch that advertisement."

She shook her head. "It's not done that way, but more by word of mouth. Miss Humphreys will probably wish to live with her brother, but we should give her a pension in her own right in case he predeceases her."

"Yes, of course."

An uneasy silence fell between them. Flora itched to pick up her embroidery but would he take this as a dismissal? Impulsively, she asked, "Would you like to read to me while I continue with my embroidery?"

Her husband seemed astonished but pleased by her request. "I should be delighted to. What would you like to hear? A novel or some poetry? Byron, perhaps?"

"Do we have Pope's *Homer* in the library?"

"I don't know. We have the original Greek, of course, but I fear I am too rusty to translate it for you extempore. Why do you want to hear it?"

"It may be too late for me to learn Greek, but I should like to know something of the literature at least. So many gentlemen like to demonstrate their superiority to us ladies by quoting an epigram or making a clever allusion which we cannot understand. If you were to read it to me, I would have a better idea of what is meant when someone refers to Circe, for example." She sighed. "I have never understood why boys and girls are educated so differently."

"Something else for us to think about when we are considering tutors and governesses." He stood. "I'll have a quick look in the library, see what I can find. If nothing comes quickly to hand, I'll have a more thorough look tomorrow."

"No, no. In fact it can wait until you are returned from Oxford, as otherwise we would have to interrupt our readings."

"True. And if we do not have a copy here, I shall look for one there. Have you another wish?"

"Yes." She held up a leather-bound volume. "Have you read any of *Otanes'* letters in *The Observer*? They are couched as the reports of the envoy of an eastern potentate to his master and throw an interesting light on our own society. Now they have all been put into one volume, together with his valedictory letter as he leaves this country to return home. I received it last week but have not yet had the opportunity to read it. Why don't you read it to me now? Here, I have opened it at the correct page."

He took the book and began, "*My Lord and Sovereign Master.*"

Chapter Twelve

Stanton and his father drove into Oxford mid-afternoon, their phaeton followed by a carriage piled with luggage and carrying both the duke's valet and the manservant who would help install Stanton in his rooms. A groom would arrive the next day with his horse.

"It's too late to call on the Dean—we shall do so tomorrow," Gracechurch said. "Let's see what sort of dinner *The Angel* can offer us."

Mr Shorland had reserved a suite of rooms including a private parlour and *The Angel's* dinner was more than adequate. Afterwards, his father settled down with a decanter of port at his elbow, but Stanton was restless after the long day in the coach and reluctant to sit tamely like an old man. He was no longer a boy, he reminded himself and once his father departed he would answer to no-one.

"I'll take a stroll—stretch my legs after sitting all day," he announced.

Gracechurch opened his mouth, and then closed it again. "Be sure to return by nine o'clock," he said mildly and returned to his *Times*.

Stanton picked up his hat and gloves and ran downstairs. After the Palladian calm of the Priory, he was overwhelmed by Oxford's soaring spires and immense Gothic buildings. As dusk fell, townspeople sought their homes while more and more gowned figures appeared in the streets, heading purposefully for the various inns and hostelries whose windows gleamed in invitation. A lamplighter toiled from lamp to lamp, his assistant steadying the ladder while he cast pools of golden light against the encroaching dark.

A stage coach drew up at *The Mitre* and two young men jumped down, calling for a porter to take charge of their traps. Stanton watched enviously as they strolled away until they disappeared into one of the colleges. How much better it would be to arrive independently, and not in his father's train. Next term, he resolved, he would be an old hand.

Tomorrow he would be introduced to Dr Hall and matriculated. Then he must order his gowns—as a nobleman, he required two, dress and undress. He would select a sober green silk for the former. Unfortunately there was nothing he could do about the gold lace or that ridiculous gold tassel on his cap. Still, his undress gown would be black like everyone else's.

A group of raucous students passed him, arguing loudly over where to go next. One wearing a ridiculously tufted black gown looked back over his shoulder then reversed his steps saying, "Good God, Stanton, is that you? I didn't realise you had come up."

"Just this afternoon." His cousin Randal, the grandson of Lady Ottilia's younger brother, was two years older than he. They had been at school together but due to the age difference were not particularly well acquainted. "How goes it, Whitbourne?"

"Tolerably, tolerably," the other replied with a world-weary air. "Aaah, beg to introduce Messrs. Wilkes, Shelby and Carruthers," he added, with a vague gesture towards his companions. "Gentlemen, my cousin, Lord Stanton."

"Your cousin, Whittie?" one exclaimed. "Are they matriculating infants now?"

"Only tufted ones," another sniggered. He attempted to make a leg. "Your servant, my lord."

"You're drunk, Shelby," Whitbourne said sharply.

Shelby swayed alarmingly. "Not drunk, just a trifle elevated!"

Carruthers, or was it Wilkes caught hold of him. "Let's get him home before he shoots the cat again."

"Oh, God, yes," his supporter drawled, linking Shelby on the other side.

"Shoot the cat?" Stanton murmured to his cousin as the trio made its unsteady way down the street.

"Cascade, cat, or cast up one's accounts when one is cut or has been carousing. To vomit from drunkenness!"

"Oh!" Stanton said distastefully.

"It happens to the best of us, but best to do it in private." Whitbourne jumped at the sudden crash accompanied by a volley of oaths. "What the devil's going on?"

"Your—er—associates swerved into the lamplighter's ladder," Stanton explained, watching amazed as the downed man surged to his feet and punched Carruthers in the face.

"Now we're in for it," Whitbourne exclaimed as Carruthers struck back. He began to run towards the combatants. "Come on, Stanton."

Stanton chased after him. People came running from all sides to join the fray; gownsmen and townsmen squaring up to one another vigorously so that within minutes the brawl had spread right across the street. Having exchanged a flurry of blows with an opponent who finally ducked away, Stanton swivelled to plant a facer on a brawny fellow. He danced away to come back again with a left hook but suddenly found himself lifted off his feet and over his opponent's hip, then slid down his back to land with a bone-jarring thump on the street.

He felt his arm gripped as he looked up at the fuzzy glow of the lamp. Suddenly all was quiet.

"Quickly," Whitbourne said. He pulled his cousin to his feet and handed him his hat.

Stanton blinked. "What?"

"The proctors are about. Where are you putting up?"

"*The Angel*." Stanton looked down in dismay at his muddy trousers, and then touched his hand gingerly to his face. His fingers were bloody. "How am I to explain this to my father?"

"What? Is the duke with you? All the better. If we are challenged, that should get us off. Here," Whitbourne thrust a handkerchief into Stanton's hand, "get the worst off with that." While Stanton obeyed, he took his other arm and began to stroll leisurely with him towards the inn, away from two severe-looking, capped and gowned gentlemen who had seized a young gownsman and were not to be deprived of their prey.

His feet propped on a footstool, Gracechurch rested his head against the high back of his chair. He hoped he had done the right thing in letting the boy explore on his own tonight. He smiled wryly. For seventeen years he had not given a thought to Stanton's welfare and now, when his son was all but grown-up and about to embark on an independent life, he worried about him.

This concern was the price of being a real parent, he supposed, but it was more than compensated for by the joy he found with his children. He could congratulate himself on being on better terms with all of them. It was easier to find common grounds with his sons, and he would continue to take an interest in Jasper now that Stanton had left the Priory. It was harder to get to know Tabitha but he would persevere. Following Flora's hint, he had included her in their riding parties, even though this meant he no longer had his wife to himself on these occasions. Still, he thought that Flora was softening towards him; he hoped so for the more he got to know her, the more he admired? Respected? Cared for her? No, loved her, dammit! When he returned to the Priory, although he would not neglect his children, he would chiefly devote his attention to his wife.

He had enjoyed reading to her. He had not come across *Otanes* before, and was impressed by the writer's insights, and although he did not agree with all of his conclusions, enjoyed discussing them with Flora who was more liberal in her views.

He opened his eyes at the sound of footsteps and male voices outside his door.

"What, back already?" he said as Stanton ushered a young man wearing a fellow-commoner's gown into the room.

"You remember Randal Whitbourne, do you not, sir?"

"Your Grace."

Gracechurch nodded acknowledgement of the newcomer's bow even as he took in his son's dishevelled state. What the devil had they been up to, he wondered, as he eyed the muddy trousers, dangling neckcloth and cut eyebrow. What should a concerned parent say? The boy moved stiffly too. He met his father's gaze with a mixture of apprehension, defiance and plea. He's afraid I'll embarrass him in front of his cousin, Gracechurch thought, as he looked from one to the other.

"Been raising the breeze, have you?"

"Not us," Whitbourne said. "But I'm no fair-weather friend. You won't catch me standing by when a chum is in a shindy."

Gracechurch sighed. "I suppose not. Are either of you hurt?"

"No worse than after a game of football at school," Stanton said and Whitbourne nodded agreement.

Gracechurch picked up a little bell and rang it. "A bottle of brandy and some glasses, Grimes," he said when his valet came in from the neighbouring bedroom, "and you might see what you can do for Lord Stanton so that he is fit to meet the Dean in the morning."

"At once, your Grace."

Gracechurch waved the young men to chairs at the table. "Sit down, the two of you. I'll spare you the jobation—at least you had the wit to avoid the proctors."

"Thanks to Whitbourne here," Stanton said. "I had no idea what he was about."

"Oh, we'll have you up to snuff in no time," his cousin said. "You have plenty of bottom, and that's what matters."

Stanton appeared flattered by this last comment. He accepted a glass of brandy from his father's valet and did not demur when the latter said, "My lord, if you would be so good," but followed him obediently into the bedchamber.

Left alone with the duke, Whitbourne was less the incipient swell and more the greenhorn. Gracechurch eyed him in silence for some moments, before saying, "I am grateful to you for retrieving the situation although I suspect that without you Stanton might never have blundered into it."

Whitbourne flushed but responded calmly, "To be fair, sir, it was bound to happen, if not tonight then on another day, and at least he was with me."

"Very true." Gracechurch considered his companion. The youngest grandson of the younger son of an earl, Whitbourne might be well connected but would very likely have to make his own way in life. He seemed sensible enough. "I don't ask you to bear-lead him but I should appreciate it if you would have an eye to him, especially in the first weeks until he finds his feet—point out the pitfalls."

"I should be happy to, sir."

"Excellent. More brandy or would you prefer coffee?"

"Coffee, if I may, sir."

"Tug that bell-pull, if you will be so good. It's twenty years since I was up. What's all the go here now?"

The next morning saw Julian and Roderick Malvin join Gracechurch and Stanton for breakfast. The two young men hit it off instantly, each glad to have the support of the other as they embarked on this new life. The next days were spent in a whirl of matriculation, introductions, especially to their tutors, consultation with a tailor regarding their gowns, the procurement of two very tolerable sets of chambers on the same staircase and the purchase of those items necessary to remedy the deficiencies of these sets, and making themselves known to the scout who served their staircase.

At last the great moment came when they could bid farewell to their seniors and enter into the glory and independence of their own apartments.

"I have never felt so *de trop* in my life," Gracechurch remarked to Julian Malvin as they emerged into the quadrangle.

"They positively itched to be rid of us," Mr Malvin agreed. "I suppose we were the same. It is strange to be back here and yet not part of it. Neither town nor gown, but that awful embarrassment, a parent—or *in loco parentis* in my case. Well, we have now discharged that duty. Which way shall we go? Town or river?"

"River by all means."

A blustery wind sent clouds scudding across the sky and raised ripples and wavelets in the Isis that did not deter the occupants of the various skiffs and wherries skimming over the water.

"Did you row when you were up, Duke?"

"Frequently. I liked the exercise and the sense of freedom. Sometimes I went with Charles Forde. He is related to you, is he not? Is he your brother-in-law?"

"It is one of those strange, family connections. He is married to my step-mother's sister, Henrietta, who is two years younger than I and came to live with us after her mother's death. Brother-in-law would best describe our relationship; he is uncle to my half-brothers and sister and his children are their cousins although my children, who are only a year or two younger, are their nephew and niece."

"I think you would need to sketch that for me," Gracechurch said with a grin. "My own family is quite straightforward by comparison."

"It suits us," Mr Malvin said, "but I think my next brother, Matthew, finds himself at a loss at present."

"In what way?"

"He seeks a purpose in life, I think. He came to Oxford with us, but I have hardly seen him. He has been visiting his old tutor. Our brother's death last year hit him hard. Then," he stopped and looked at Gracechurch, "it is easier for us eldest sons—our path in life is laid down for us. At times we might kick against the traces but we know we shall have a meaningful role in life as head of the family and, as peers, have a seat in the House of Lords. Younger sons do not have that assurance; on the contrary they know that they will lose their home on the day their brother comes to the title. And yet, with few exceptions, they are not expected to work for a living. If they have no taste for the military or the church, how are they to occupy themselves?"

"Politics perhaps or a government office?"

"If either interests them. This is the dilemma Matthew faces. He does not have a passion that will satisfy him such as Charles Forde has for his music, and now must ask himself what will. He is very close to our younger sister, Arabella, but my wife feels she is now ready to take a husband. If— when that happens, Matthew runs the risk of becoming one of society's bachelors—you know the sort, Bond Street loungers, who divide their time between the clubs and the ball-rooms."

"He might marry and settle down."

Mr Malvin shook his head. "I think he must find himself first. If it had not been for Arthur, my father would probably have had a word with him last year. When I came down from Oxford, he told me he would let me have my head until I was twenty-five but he would expect me to settle down to harness then. And so I did. I was ready to, what's more. But, as I said, it is easier for eldest sons."

"Yes. My own son, Jasper, will be faced with the same dilemma. He will not want financially, of course, but I do not want him to end up like my father's younger brother. The last that I heard of him, he was living abroad with a new mistress."

"That is precisely what I don't want for Matthew."

"I have been thinking, Malvin, that the education we offer our sons is too restricted, confined as it is chiefly to the classics. We need to expand their horizons both metaphorically and literally."

"We have lost the custom of sending them on the Grand Tour."

"It could be revived, but I think that is too late. *The child is father of the man*, as the poet Wordsworth has it. We should encourage them to discover their natural talents and interests at a younger age."

"You are right. I might encourage Matthew to travel for a year or so—he was in Brussels with my parents in '14, but from what I could gather, they moved very much in English society while they were there."

"If Europe does not appeal, he might like to look further east. Or would he be interested in joining an Embassy? I could have a word with Castlereagh."

"I have no idea."

"Why don't you and he dine with me when we are back in town? I am not without influence, if there is something that appeals to him."

"That is very kind of you, Duke."

Gracechurch was not given to patronage. He had rarely interested himself enough in another person to secure a favour or a position for him. But he had enjoyed talking to Julian Malvin as one parent to another, considering what might be best for their offspring. He would do better by Jasper than he had by Stanton. Not that he would neglect Stanton from now on, of course, but his support must be more subtle. And his daughter needed him. He had winced when Flora told him of Tabitha's desire to 'have a gentleman of their own' on joint outings with the Rembletons. But there was no point repining over the wasted past—he must look to a better future.

Chapter Thirteen

"They're gone," Tabitha said gloomily as Stanton guided the phaeton down the avenue. "What are we to do now?"

"What we always did," Jasper said. "It's back to the schoolroom for us." He sounded just as glum as his sister.

"We cannot declare every day a holiday," Flora pointed out. "Then a holiday would be nothing special, would it?"

"Perhaps not—but it's so dashed boring with no other fellows to talk to."

Tabitha sniffed. "Well, I don't want to talk to a great rudesby like you either."

"Enough! If the two of you cannot speak civilly to one another, I am sure we can find some task for you to complete in silence. An essay on politeness, perhaps." As her children looked at each other, appalled, Flora added, "And, if you wish to have more holidays while the Rembletons are here, you would be wise to ensure that you are not behindhand with any of your lessons."

"Yes, Mamma," came the doleful chorus.

"Now, in you go."

"Yes, Mamma." Tabitha turned to obey and then looked back. "You will dine with us today, will you not, and sleep in the old house again?"

"Yes, my love. I will."

But schoolroom dinner taken with her old governess and her younger children seemed dull and insipid after ten days of more adult company. Worse, instead of being glad to be back in the tranquility of her own bedroom, she found she missed the private chats with her husband as well as his goodnight kiss. Too restless to sleep, Flora sat for a long time looking out into the moonlit garden.

Drat the man! He had succeeded in breaching her defences. And not only hers. She was not the only one to be considered. If he—if she—if they—what changes would be necessary in the way they lived, both here and in town? If she were to spend more time with her husband, what would it mean for the children, for Tabitha in particular? Would it be fair to her—or to Miss Humphreys—if they were to be left much more to their own devices? If she were to move permanently to the duchess's apartments, should they remain in the old house? It was like a game of spillikins—remove one stick and you risked collapsing the whole edifice. And who knew how long Jeffrey's change of heart would last? That was the greatest question of all. Which husband would return from Oxford—the new or the old?

In the meantime, she must plan for Olivia's visit. She would return to the duchess's apartments, of course. Should she give Olivia different rooms to those she had been used to share with her late husband? No, it wasn't necessary—after all the Fitzmaurices had spent the winter in Olivia's home, Southrode Manor. Clearly Mr Fitzmaurice had no qualms about filling a dead man's shoes.

Mr Rembleton had always taken the children for a ramble on the morning of May Eve, encouraging them to note the various signs of spring in the notebooks they kept just for this purpose, a notebook he ceremoniously presented to each child once they were able to write. Tabitha had been just five, she remembered. On this expedition, the budding naturalists visited a variety of habitats, as they had learnt to call them, including a search for frogspawn or tadpoles, and they invariably returned blissfully muddy, and in dire need of sustenance.

Perhaps she should suggest that they resume the tradition. Between them, John Rembleton and Jasper would be able to lead the little group to the various locations under the supervision of Jeffrey and Mr Fitzmaurice. It would remove the children from underfoot while the schoolroom was dismantled so that the Great Hall could be prepared for the May Eve guests.

"I have the two girls together, and John and Jasper are together, but what about Samuel?" Flora said to Miss Humphreys the next morning. "He is six now, too young to put him in with the boys, but I think the girls may prefer to be on their own."

"There is that little powder room between Miss Mullins' room and mine," the governess suggested. "It has been used as a linen-press since powdering went out of fashion, but if the shelves are taken down, it should be possible to put in a truckle bed and a chair and table. If Miss Mullins leaves the door on her side unlocked, Samuel can call to her if he needs her."

"An excellent idea. I'll talk to Podmore and the carpenter, see if it can be done in time. I'll do it now, before I forget. Would you be so good as to ring the bell?"

"Certainly, but—your Grace, may I first have a moment of your time?"

"Why, is something wrong?" Flora was alarmed by this formal request. "Have the children been up to mischief?"

"No, it is not that. If I might sit?"

"Please. Here." Flora hastily pulled out a chair and took one opposite it. "Miss Humphreys, are you feeling quite well?"

"I am well enough—just getting old. I am three-and-sixty now, and to be frank, I find it increasingly difficult to keep up with a lively and quick-witted girl like Lady Tabitha. She needs a younger instructress, one who is more *au courant* with the manners and styles of today and who will be better able than I to prepare her for her exalted station in life. I have been thinking about this since Miss Mullins and the children stayed with us last autumn after Mr and Mrs Fitzmaurice's wedding. I was most impressed by Miss Mullins but cannot deny that her way of dealing with her pupils is different to mine. She is better informed and much more active." Miss Humphreys dabbed at her eyes with her handkerchief. "I get so tired, Flora. I need my quiet time. I find the days get longer and longer and I long for bed."

Flora gently took the wrinkled hand of her old governess. "I understand. I cannot tell you how much I honour you that you recognise this. I know you have always put your pupils first."

"I have tried. It was easy here at Stanton, especially when they were your children. I was so grateful when you asked me to come to you. It is not easy to find a position when one is over fifty. But now it is time for me to retire from my post. I have some savings—"

"As to that, you will always be part of this family and the duke and I will see that you are never in want. We will be happy to arrange for a cottage and a pension for you, either here or elsewhere. I imagine you would like to remain near your brother."

"Of course. We have talked about it, Tobias and I. Last Sunday he said in jest that we should take Miss Fortescue's cottage and have Jane look after us there. It is quite snug, you see, not like that great, draughty rectory that was built for a large family and is far too big for a single man. He would be happy to give the curate the lion's share of the income and just keep for himself what we would need, he said."

"I am sure that something could be arranged. Let us discuss it again after May Eve. Now I really must talk to Podmore before the music master comes. I'll sit with Tabitha during the lesson and I want you to lie down on your bed for an hour. Don't worry, please, dear Miss Humphreys. It will all come right, I promise you."

She had better write to her husband, Flora thought as she waited for the housekeeper. If Mr Humphreys truly decided to assume the curate's role, they would need a more experienced man for the rectory. A married man too, she decided, preferably with a family. Gracechurch would need to know.

"I do not need to ask if you are happy," Flora said the next afternoon when she and Olivia had retreated to Flora's dressing-room. The children were busy renewing their acquaintance and Mr Fitzmaurice had tactfully claimed that he needed an hour to finish reading some papers. "After that, I am completely at your disposal, Duchess."

"You are positively blooming," Flora said as she handed her friend a cup of tea.

"In every sense," Olivia said, a mischievous glint in her eye.

"What? Are you with child?"

"I am almost certain. It has been eight weeks. Luke knows, but nobody else."

"He took to fatherhood so well that I am sure he is over the moon."

Olivia sighed. "Yes, when he is not fussing and cosseting me. No matter how often I remind him that I have already borne three children without difficulty, he retorts that it is the first time for him."

Flora wondered how Gracechurch would react if she were to conceive again. She remembered his sudden pallor when they had learnt of Tommy's errand. Had he for a moment re-lived his daughter's death? Perhaps he would prefer not to have any more children—but he had never taken even the most obvious of precautions to prevent it. Except, he had not come to her bed since expressing his desire to have a closer connection with her. Perhaps he sought a chaster, more companionate marriage now. Was that what he meant by friendship? But if that were so, he would not kiss her at every opportunity, would he?

"And what of you, Flora? You seem a little *distraite*."

She sighed. "To be frank, I feel like the old woman who was tossed up in a basket, Olivia. So much has happened this last month that I do not know if I am on my head or my heels."

"Good heavens!" Olivia came to sit on the sopha and took Flora's hand. "You know you may tell me anything, Flora. Heaven knows, we have shared enough confidences and worries over the years."

Flora took a deep breath. "You know that Gracechurch and I live more or less parallel lives, even during the few weeks each year that we find ourselves under the same roof. You have spent enough weeks in Gracechurch House to know that our daily lives rarely intersect—far less than yours and Mr Rembleton did."

"I suppose that is true. Certainly, Jack took more of an interest in the children than Gracechurch ever did."

"So you may imagine how startled I was to receive a letter in Gracechurch's own hand and with his seal. I cannot remember when he last wrote to me—probably when Tabitha was born. Otherwise, if there is something he wishes me to know, he has his secretary pen a note. I must have stared at the seal for a full quarter of an hour before breaking it. He wrote perfectly civilly to say that he was removing Stanton from Harrow because he wanted him to go up to Oxford with the Malvins' youngest son."

"I had not thought he was on such terms with the Malvins that that would be important to him."

"Nor I. But not only that, he said he would collect Stanton from Harrow, bring him here for the vacation and take him to Oxford himself and see him settled there. That is where they are now."

"That is certainly strange. Is it because he suddenly realised that Stanton is all but adult now?"

"I thought that at first but then, the evening he arrived here, he came and begged my pardon for having been inconsiderate, even negligent, both as a husband and a father and said he wished to make amends."

Olivia's jaw dropped. "He what? Are you sure he is not ill?"

Flora laughed. "I asked him that as well. He said, no, he had had a sudden insight."

"Like St Paul on the road to Damascus?"

"A bit."

"Good heavens! One reads of people experiencing sudden conversions, but one does not expect to encounter it in one's own family. Has he changed his behaviour?"

"He certainly spends more time with us—with me and the children. He gave Stanton driving and fencing lessons, and invited me to accompany him when he rode out. And he joins us for lunch most days."

"What, in the small house? I thought he never went there."

"The day he and Stanton arrived, we went out to meet them, well to meet Stanton, I suppose. I had gone back into the house with Tabitha when for some reason Jasper invited his father to come and eat a hot cross bun in the schoolroom. To my utter astonishment, he came. Although he did go first to the old schoolroom, Stanton told me."

"Did he comment on the new one?"

"Not really. But it was not long before Tabitha let the cat out of the bag."

"In what way?"

"*Mamma only goes to the duchess's apartments when you come. Usually, she stays here with us,*" Flora quoted in her daughter's didactic tones and then dissolved into laughter. "The look on your face, Olivia!"

"Well, I'm 'fair flabbergasted', as my brother would say. What did Gracechurch do?"

"He—stiffened but said nothing. Nor did I. Then Tabitha said she must finish her piano practice, making it clear she expected him to remain and listen to her."

"I can just picture her doing so," Olivia said appreciatively. "Did he stay?"

"Yes, and behaved as politely as if he were in a *ton* drawing-room. But he made his escape immediately afterwards. Later, before dinner, he came in here and said he wanted to talk to me. That was when he apologised."

"It's no wonder you are *distraite*. You must not have known what to say."

"Not at first. But then I was furious. He experiences this change of heart and we are all expected to—to accommodate him. He is suddenly calling me Flora. I haven't heard my name on his lips since he made his marriage vows. It was always Lady Stanton, and then Duchess. And then, which was truly sad, he could not decide which of his Christian names I should use. He does not have a particular connection to any of them, it appears."

"As if he has no sense of his inner self?"

"Exactly. I could not but feel for him, Olivia. And he does seem to sincerely wish to change his ways. But must I change mine too?"

"You may not have much choice. One change will inevitably force another."

"Now Gracechurch wants to make the saloon between our apartments more cosy, so that we can be private there."

"That sounds as if he intends to spend more time here. Perhaps he will also want you to spend more time in town."

"But why should I? Why should I uproot myself and the children just because of his whim? Who knows how long it will last?"

"Only you can decide how far you are willing to facilitate him. I will not preach to you of your duty, for I do not think you owe him any. You must think first of your own happiness, even before that of the children. But, Flora, change will come—indeed has come already. And perhaps that is no bad thing. You are still a young woman with half your life before you. Have you really been content with the way you live?"

"I made myself be," Flora said quietly. She sighed. "And if that wasn't enough, yesterday Miss Humphreys told me she is growing old and fears she can no longer cope with Tabitha, and Jasper is to go to Harrow in September."

"And Stanton is no longer a schoolboy," Olivia said quietly. "Your house has come tumbling down around you, has it not?"

"Yes. I have no choice but to rebuild. I suppose it will be easier to make changes if we have a new governess. But in another ten years, the children will have grown up. Even Tabitha. And what then?"

"Your circumstances are similar to what mine were. But one thing I will say, Flora, is that while Gracechurch and Jack may have been distant, they were never violent or tyrannical or lacked respect in any way, nor did they abuse the rights the law gives husbands."

"That is true."

"In fact, they left us a lot of freedom. I never had to worry that Jack would countermand my orders or question my decisions. Even when he appointed Gracechurch as co-trustee, he made it clear that that was only so he could serve as a bulwark between me and Jack's brother."

"Gracechurch has never interfered with me here either, but that may be because he had not realised to what extent I work together with his steward. Just this last week, he said he was ashamed that he was unaware of it."

"What have you to lose if you give him a chance to prove himself?"

My heart. The words rose unbidden from Flora's inmost depths, and aghast, she pressed her fingers against her lips to force them back. *No, not that. She did not want that.*

When she remained silent, Olivia asked gently, "Are you afraid? I was, you know, with Luke. When you have been deprived of intimacy for so long, the prospect of it is terrifying. I do not mean physical intimacy, you understand. It is an intimacy of the heart and soul. *Then I shall know, even as also I am known,"* she quoted. "And yet, when you find that mutual deep trust with another, it is indescribably beautiful."

"But I would have to put my whole self at risk."

"So must he—indeed, if he is sincere, he already has done so. Now you must see if he keeps his promises. If it is only a whim, it will dissipate quickly enough."

"I suppose you are right. I thought of asking him to take the children on a nature ramble on Tuesday morning."

"That would certainly put him to the test," Olivia said with a faint smile. "They have very definite ideas of how it is to be done. If Gracechurch balks at the idea, I am sure Luke will be happy to oblige you. Samuel will need a notebook. I shall ask John to help him with the headings tomorrow."

Chapter Fourteen

Had she been entirely fair to her husband, Flora wondered as Merle brushed out her hair and dressed it again for the evening. If truth were told, he had probably been less willing than she to enter into their marriage. On the other hand, he had been the elder and much more experienced. But what was done was done. He was a very reserved man. What courage must it have taken to expose himself so to her, to put himself at her mercy? And, as Olivia pointed out, leaving his distance out of the equation, he had always treated her fairly.

Of course, she had never put him to the test. She wondered fleetingly what would have happened if she had—if she had developed a taste for gambling or a, a lech for some poet like poor Lady Caroline Lamb had had for Byron.

Supposing Gracechurch had discovered she had been the inspiration behind the mysterious Muses at Watier's famous masquerade. The beau monde had tried for weeks to identify the identically clad and masked dancers who had later flirted outrageously, flitting from gentleman to gentleman. Buoyed by the exhilaration of the dance, she had enjoyed several brief encounters but none of her admirers could tempt her to seek out a private space for more intimate dalliance. Was she too strait-laced to respond or had all natural instincts faded during her loveless marriage? And would Gracechurch have cared if he knew she had been among that disreputable throng?

She frowned as the maid adjusted the silk turban so that it sat perfectly on her dark curls. The celestial blue brought out the colour of her eyes, but she looked very pale.

"A touch of rouge, Merle, as well as the lip salve." She tilted her head to let the maid brush the powder over her cheeks. "That's better. Thank you. That will be all."

Flora returned to her musings. Olivia had been a byword among the *ton* for austere rectitude—an icicle, one rejected swain had called her. No-one could doubt that she had found true happiness with Mr Fitzmaurice. And she had been terrified of intimacy, she said.

"Enough!" she said aloud, checked her appearance one last time in the cheval glass and left the room. She must be in the drawing-room before her guests arrived.

Tabitha leaned on the arm of the sopha and whispered, "Mamma?"

"What is it, dearest?"

"When will his Grace return?"

"I don't know exactly on which day, but he promised he would be here by May Eve."

"But that's not until Tuesday—another four days. And the Rembletons can't stay as long as usual this year because of Mr Fitzmaurice going to Parliament, they said." The girl's lip trembled. "I thought this year we could show them that we have a father who does things with us too."

"I'm sure you will be able to, dearest. But first he must make sure that your brother is settled at Oxford. Now, you and Miranda must be sure to include Jasper in your games sometimes. Remember how you didn't like it when John and Stanton left you out."

"Yes, Mamma."

"The Noah's Ark is in the toy chest under the window. See if he would like to help you put the animals in the right order."

The other children drifted over as soon as Tabitha began to set out the pieces and it wasn't long before Flora heard her say firmly, "If you put the lions and the antelopes together, the lions will eat the antelopes."

"But what did the lions and tigers eat if they couldn't eat the other animals?" Samuel wanted to know.

There was a pause while the four older children looked at each other, then John said, "Fish, maybe, or crocodiles. They can swim so they wouldn't have to go into the ark."

When Mr Fitzmaurice squatted down to inspect the arrangement, Olivia came to sit beside Flora.

"This reminds me of the first time we came to dinner at Gracechurch House. Jack got down onto the floor to play with Stanton. So much has happened since then, and yet it is only twelve years ago. I don't know if I ever thanked you properly." Her face softened as she looked at her new husband. "It is only now that I realise what a bleak existence I might have led without you. I might never have found my feet in the *ton* nor had the courage to make a satisfactory life for myself."

"Nonsense. It might have taken a little longer, but that is all. I am so pleased that you came as usual for May Eve, and that Mr Fitzmaurice came with you."

"Even had I not wished to come, the children would have insisted. They are determined to maintain all our traditions including the outing to Hampton Court. John keeps reminding me that we didn't go last year because of Waterloo and this may be his last opportunity before he goes to school."

Although the children were engrossed in their game, Flora lowered her voice. "Gracechurch wonders whether Harrow is the best choice for Jasper but I am not sure what alternative there is."

"Does he indeed? Luke is not convinced of the wisdom of sending boys to school either, especially an intelligent boy like John who is accustomed to discussing matters rationally with his instructors. He thinks with the right tutors they would do much better at home. It should be possible to engage supplementary instructors in the sciences while we are in town and as they get older they could attend talks at the Royal Society for example."

"Perhaps we should arrange something together," Flora said. "It would be more interesting for John and Jasper than sitting alone in their own schoolrooms."

"Have a sort of peregrinatory school, you mean?"

"Why not, especially if we could convince other parents to join with us. They need to associate with other boys."

"Why should they not have some classes at least with their sisters too? But this topic is for another day, Flora. What I want to say now is this; Jack had his own secrets that prevented any possibility of a different, closer connection between us. If that is not the case with Gracechurch, then I think you should at least consider his plea. I'll say no more," Olivia added hastily as the drawing-door opened to admit Lady Ottilia and Mr Harte, "but know that you may talk to me at any time."

Jasper manipulated the strings of a kite while John ran ahead holding the yard-long construction of silk and wood aloft until the wind caught it and tugged it out of his grasp, sending it high above them.

"Huzza!" Jasper ran whooping over the lawn, hastily letting out more string as the kite soared even higher. "Look, Mamma!"

"Well done!" she called, then jumped when someone touched her shoulder.

"Flora." Her husband stood smiling at her.

She smiled back and held out her hands, surprised by how pleased she was to see him. "Welcome home, Jeffrey. I had not expected you today."

He retained her hands and stooped to kiss her cheek. "Stanton and young Malvin could not wait to be rid of us. They have taken adjoining sets of chambers on the same staircase and were busy primping their quarters when I left."

"You must tell me all about it. Have they ordered their gowns?"

"We went directly from the Dean to the tailor."

"What colour silk did Stanton choose in the end?"

"Dark green—it looks well with the gold. You would have smiled to see him pretend not to preen while he strove to catch sight of himself in every possible glass."

"It must be rather splendid. I should love to see him in all his glory. I shall ask him to put it on for me when he comes home. What else did they do?"

"They've met their tutors and spent last night under their own roofs, while the Malvins and I remained at *The Angel.* Is all well here?"

"Yes, indeed."

"When did the Fitzmaurices arrive?"

"Yesterday." She gestured towards the two boys. "John had apparently promised to bring his kite and show Jasper how to fly it."

"Mind the trees, Jasper," John called anxiously. "If it gets caught at the top of one, we shall never be able to get it down."

Suddenly, the kite swooped low. "Hold on!" John shouted, running towards Jasper, then, "Watch out, sir!"

Gracechurch ducked instinctively as the kite plummeted towards him but was too late to avoid the collision that swept his hat from his head. He spun around to confront his crestfallen son whose evident mortification and valiant attempt not to laugh had Gracechurch's own lips twitching.

"I beg your pardon, sir; I did not mean to do it."

"I am relieved to hear it," Gracechurch said dryly, "although if you had, I should be compelled to admire your dexterity."

"For a first attempt at flying one, it was not too bad," John said as he rewound the kite-string. "You lost the wind when you turned. Do you want to try again, Jasper?"

"Start further from the trees," Gracechurch recommended, "and we shall take ourselves out of danger." He grinned at his wife who had retrieved his hat and now handed it to him.

Flora tucked her hand into Gracechurch's arm. "Let us join the others." She nodded towards where Samuel Rembleton ran ahead of his mother and stepfather, bowling his hoop. Tabitha and Miranda skipped along behind them, skirts, sashes and ribbons fluttering as they gracefully turned their ropes over their heads in preparation for the next jump. "I hope you received my note about the Humphreys in time to prevent you offering the curacy to some young candidate?"

"I did, thank you, but I would not have done so without arranging for you to meet him first."

"How does one select a rector? When you think about it, we may have to live with the new man for upwards of thirty years, listen to his sermons; if we choose badly, endure his moralising—"

"When you put it like that, you frighten me. What should we look for?"

"He must be intelligent and a good speaker but not one of your fashionable preachers. Sincere in his religion without…"

"Being sanctimonious," he suggested.

"Yes, or pompous. Someone we are happy to see at our table—not unctuous, a gentleman, but one who is willing minister to all his parishioners, not just the gentry."

"And not neglect the glebe in favour of squeezing the last penny from the tithes."

"He should have a wife who will support him in all his endeavours, and perhaps daughters who would be companions for Tabitha. Oh dear, where are we going to find such paragons?"

"We cannot rush into this, but should take our time to make some discreet enquiries when we are in town. Julian Malvin and I discussed the plight of younger sons who have no obvious purpose in life. Perhaps if we could find the right one—"

"Perhaps—but we must make clear that he may not be an absentee who installs a curate to do all the work."

"This will delay setting up your school."

"It can't be helped. And if we get the right man, he can do it. I don't mean act as schoolmaster, but consider where we might find one. I must ask Olivia what they do at Southrode. And of course we must think about a new governess, and perhaps a tutor for Jasper. Olivia and I were talking about that too."

"How long do the Fitzmaurices stay?"

"They leave on the second. Parliament is sitting again Olivia says, and Mr Fitzmaurice does not want to tarry. What about you? Are you anxious to return to town?"

He stopped and placed his hand over hers where it rested on his arm. "My return to town depends on you. I shall remain here until you are ready to come with me. You are my chief interest now, and the children, of course. Everything and everyone else can go hang!"

"Jeffrey!"

"Flora!"

Before she knew what he was about, he had ducked in under the brim of her bonnet and kissed her. Her lips trembled under his, clinging for a moment before she pulled away.

"Jeffrey!" Her hand seemed to rise of its own volition to touch his cheek.

"What are you doing? Why did you kiss Mamma?"

Flora felt her cheeks grow warm and she hastily dropped her hand, grateful that Tabitha had addressed her question to her father rather than to her mother. Jeffrey seemed in no case to answer her, but Miranda Rembleton came to his rescue.

"Married people do that," she explained importantly to her friend. "At least—I don't remember Papa Jack very well but Papa Fitz kisses Mamma all the time."

"Miranda!"

Now it was Mrs Fitzmaurice's turn to blush but her husband just laughed and said, "Miranda has the right of it. It is a husband's privilege."

"We were discussing when we should leave for town, Olivia," Flora said in an effort to change the subject. "There is bound to be a drawing-room after Princess Charlotte's nuptials and we shall have to attend."

"Do you think we must go too? I had to be presented again after Luke and I were married but Lady Lutterworth did it while presenting her new daughter-in-law at the last drawing-room."

"You were the first lady I presented."

"How long ago that is. I was petrified, I remember, but you were so composed and poised that I took my example from you and pretended I was a duchess too."

"So that was the secret of the haughty Mrs Rembleton," Mr Fitzmaurice said with a teasing smile for his wife. "A duchess in spirit, looking down her arrogant nose at lesser mortals."

Olivia raised an eyebrow. "She has not forgotten how to do so, sir."

"And there she is again." He shot the others an unrepentant grin. "I was used to play a private game, see if I could provoke her into giving me a set-down; it was a point to me if I succeeded."

"Luke! It is well for you that I do not have a fan with me."

"What was the final score?" Gracechurch asked, visibly amused.

"The best possible—love-all," the other man said promptly, raising his wife's hand to his lips. "Love cancels all scores."

It's as simple as that, Flora thought, and as terrifying.

Tabitha raised her rope again. "I'm going to see if I can skip thirty times without stopping."

"That will take a lot of breath. Would it help if I count for you?" Gracechurch asked.

Yes, please, Pap—" She broke off, biting her lip.

He squatted in front of her so that she could look into his eyes. "Papa? Would you like to call me Papa?"

She nodded vigorously.

"I should be happy if you did. I am your Papa, am I not?"

She threw her arms around his neck. "Now you are my Papa. Before you weren't, not really."

He rose to his feet as he hugged her back. "Then I am sorry for it. Will you forgive me?"

She nodded again and he kissed her cheek before setting her down carefully. She smiled brilliantly at him, then picked up her rope and held it in the starting position.

"Are you ready? Off you go!" His eyes fixed on his daughter, Gracechurch carefully counted the loops as she brought the rope over her head and down to jump over it— "twenty-seven, twenty-eight, twenty-nine, thirty. Excellently done, Sweeting!"

Her face lit up and she slipped her hand into his, chattering about everything that had happened in his absence as they continued towards the house. He listened with every appearance of attention, throwing in the odd question or comment to keep the flow going.

Jasper paced beside him, clearly waiting for his sister to draw breath. At last he was able to beg permission to show his father's new equipage to his friend. Mr Fitzmaurice declared his intention of coming too and the gentlemen and children veered off towards the stables.

"Mr Fitzmaurice takes his duties as stepfather very seriously," Flora said as she handed Olivia a cup of tea. "Did you find it difficult to—share your children with him?"

"No—not at all. There were some incidences in the beginning where they tried to pit one of us against the other, but Luke explained to them that that was not fair play. Like Jack, he does not talk down to them, and they like that."

"I was intrigued to hear Miranda refer to Mr Rembleton as 'Papa Jack'."

"We encourage them to talk about him—we do not want them to forget him—and this seemed the most logical approach. I don't recall who said it first. And John is happy to call Luke 'Papa Fitz', while 'Papa Fitzmaurice', which was Miranda's original idea, was too childish for him. I imagine he will drop 'Papa' altogether in a couple of years and just say 'Fitz'. But, talking of husbands and fathers, the change in Gracechurch is truly remarkable. I should not have believed it if I had not seen it. He is a different man."

"He says it is as if he went through life wearing blinkers, seeing but not perceiving."

"And experienced a sudden change of heart."

"It is very strange. The children seem to have accepted it quite easily, and I am glad for them of course—"

"But what of you? He clearly wants to put his marriage on a different footing as well."

"Yes. He would like us to be friends, he says."

Olivia raised an eyebrow. "Friends? A platonic friendship, you mean?"

Flora sighed. "I don't know, Olivia. He came the Saturday before Easter, and was here until Monday when he took Stanton to Oxford but although he spent hours with me—and the children—during the day, and we sat together in the evenings after everyone else had left the drawing-room, he never came to my bed, which he generally does when we are under the same roof. Usually on the second night and sometimes once again before he leaves."

"How is he there? Quite ardent or more—expeditious?"

When Flora just stared at her, Olivia said, "Expeditious, I take it."

"I suppose so. I have no means of comparison."

"No, of course not. If he wishes to make a change, he may not be sure how to go about it."

"What do you mean?"

"Well, what does he usually do?" When Flora gaped at her, she continued, "I mean does he silently get into bed or does he say something first. How do you know that is what he wants?"

"He comes into my room, carrying a branch of candles. He puts it down on the table and asks if he may join me."

"And then?"

"I say yes, he takes off his dressing gown and gets into bed. I pull up my nightgown and open my legs and he, well, he does it."

"Expeditiously."

"Expeditiously."

"Supposing you change the game a little, see what happens?"

"Do you mean I should refuse him? I rarely have—only if I had my courses or once or twice if I was otherwise unwell."

"Perhaps not reject him outright unless you cannot bear the thought of congress. But delay things. Allow him to join you but don't immediately—prepare for boarders, shall we say?"

Flora spluttered and hastily put down her cup. "You have been spending too much time with your brother, the admiral."

"It is not easy to find the words to discuss these matters. I will only say, Flora, that duty is a poor bedfellow, compared with inclination and affection."

"Olivia, is it really so different? After all, the— fundamentals do not change, do they?"

"Yes and no. It is like a song or other piece of music. The melody may stay the same, but each composer will harmonise differently and every musician brings his or her own talent and accomplishment and passion to it."

Flora eyed the younger woman who smiled to herself, dreamy-eyed, and repressed the urge to enquire about Mr Fitzmaurice's accomplishments, which, she recalled, were highly spoken of by certain *ton* matrons.

"So what should I do?"

"Follow his lead, for now at any rate, but also your own instincts. Don't suppress your feelings or your reactions—there are no rules and no right or wrong, only what pleases."

"But, Olivia, supposing he does want a platonic friendship? I don't think I could bear it if I—beckoned him in and he shut the door in my face."

"I understand," Olivia said slowly. "Could you see yourself at least unlocking the door? It is then up to him to try the handle."

"Perhaps. What do you mean?"

"He has just returned from Oxford; if he follows his usual pattern, he should come to you tomorrow night."

"Yes."

"He does not wake you, does he?"

"No, never."

"So presumably he does not wait very long after you have retired."

"I suppose not. I never thought of that, but no."

"Then why don't you sit up reading instead of getting directly into bed tomorrow night. See how he reacts to the changed situation?"

"And if he doesn't come?"

"Try it again the next night. One thing I will say, Flora; is that did not look like a platonic kiss earlier in the Park."

Olivia had left Flora more puzzled than ever. It was all very well for her, Flora had pointed out. She had found happiness with a new husband; they had started with a clean slate. That must have been simpler than trying to rewrite your marriage with a husband of almost twenty years.

Olivia had not denied it. As they parted on the first floor landing, she had said, "Remember, you have already begun this new volume. Do you want to tear it up and return to the end of the previous one?"

Lose the newfound ease and intimacy between her and Jeffrey? Everything in her resisted the suggestion. "No," she had replied slowly, "I don't want that."

"Then you have no choice but to go on."

Chapter Fifteen

Jeffrey could not remember a happier day than today. Arriving at Stanton to see the children playing under the trees, he had impulsively handed the reins to his groom and struck across the lawns to join his wife. She had greeted him with the most beautiful smile and outstretched hands, her cheek tilted to receive his kiss. "Welcome home, Jeffrey," she had said. He was home at last.

He had had to kiss her again when he saw her expression of joyful astonishment after he told her that his return to town depended on her.

He smiled to himself, remembering Tabitha's comment and Miranda's reply; "Married people do that". The children's remarks never failed to delight him, they were so honest and they saw things so clearly. He felt again the solid weight of Tabitha as he lifted her, her arms around his neck, heard her accolade; "Now you are my Papa."

He had a family, even friends. Mr Shorland had taken a week's leave and so Jeffrey and Flora could dine alone with the Fitzmaurices. It had been a pleasant evening, with the conversation ranging from private to public matters and back again. They had just talked—there had been no need for music or cards or any other entertainment—the long, close friendship between the two ladies noticeable in a tone of congenial informality that both gentlemen were happy to adopt.

To his surprise, Jeffrey had found himself enlisted together with Fitzmaurice to escort the children on a nature ramble on the morning of May Eve. On his protesting that he knew very little about nature, he had been informed that such erudition was not necessary. John and Jasper knew what to look for, having accompanied John's father on several such excursions. "If they discover anything new, they may consult Mr Rembleton's *Encyclopaedia*," Flora said.

"And if that fails, they may write to Mr Wilkins," Mrs Fitzmaurice added. "John is in regular correspondence with him. All that is required of you gentlemen is to dampen any excessive ardour when it comes to climbing trees or anything of that nature, fish them out of the stream if they fall in and see that they return by two o'clock."

"What about the girls and Samuel?" Jeffrey enquired. "Do they come too?"

"Yes. It will be too much for Miss Humphreys," Flora said, "but Miss Mullins will accompany you. We'll send a groom with a gig to the half-way point so that she may return with the girls or Samuel should they tire."

"May I hope your cook will supply us with sufficient provisions, Duchess?" Mr Fitzmaurice asked. "I do not see John and Jasper lasting all morning without additional sustenance."

Jeffrey took a steadying breath and opened the door to his wife's bedchamber. The candles were lit, the curtains around the big four-poster bed drawn back and the bed clothes turned down but of Flora there was no sign. He hesitated, then placed the candelabrum he carried on a table and crossed the room. He tapped on the dressing-room door before opening it.

Wrapped in pale peach silk, Flora sat at her dressing table, her maid behind her and slightly to one side. When the woman saw Jeffrey, she looked at her mistress for instructions.

"That will be all, Merle. Good night."

"Good night, your Grace." The maid quietly put down her hairbrush and slipped out of the room.

The servants' door clicked shut and Flora turned slowly to face him, the silence stretching between them. "I had not expected you," she said for the second time that day, but now there was no welcoming smile or outstretched hands. She looked apprehensive; her wide eyes, black in the candlelight, emphasised her pallor, as did the cloud of dark hair that framed her face and tumbled down her back.

So had she looked on their wedding-night, he remembered, only then she already lay against the pillows, the bride passively awaiting consummation. He swallowed. "Should I go?"

An even longer silence, then, "Yes—no—I don't know."

To his horror, her eyes filled with tears. He had her in his arms before he heard the whispered, "I can't do this, Jeffrey."

If she had not called him by his name, he would have left her then, bowed to her decision. But now, he could not. "You do not have to do anything you do not wish to do," he said soothingly, leading her to the day-bed. "Come, sit here with me and tell me what distresses you so. What is it you cannot do?"

Her breath hitched. "My marriage duty."

He looked down at her bent head. Duty was all it had ever been to her, and whose fault was that?

She wiped her eyes on a silk sleeve. "Before, all I had to do was allow you but now—I don't know what you want—what I should do." Her voice trailed away. She sounded sixteen again.

He rocked her gently. "Hush, my darling, don't cry. I have been a poor husband to you, I own, and if any duty is owed between us, it is from me to you." He gently smoothed her hair back from her face. "I have not seen you with your hair down since our wedding day. Will you allow me to try and turn the clock back, and start anew?"

"How?"

"By first getting to know you so that we may be comfortable with each other. I should have said then, 'Don't be frightened, Flora. We will take our time and I will do nothing you do not like. Whether we truly become man and wife tonight or in some weeks' time—it does not matter.'"

She twisted to look at him. "But would people not have noticed—the sheets, I mean?"

He smiled at her. "There are ways of dealing with that, if necessary."

"Oh. You must think I am very ignorant."

He shook his head. "Innocent, perhaps, as we all once were. I was careless of you. I am sorry. I should have held you like this and said, 'Tell me about yourself'. You never have, have you? Talked about your life before, about your parents? They had died not long before, had they not?"

"Yes. And my brother and sister—Charlie was five years older than I, and Tabbie three. My mother's father had died and they all went to the funeral except me; I was recovering from the measles—the others had had them before I was born—and so had to remain at home with Miss Humphreys. Mamma promised she would take me to Weymouth for the sea-bathing when they returned.

"But Grandfather had succumbed to a virulent fever that proved highly contagious. By the time they arrived there, the whole household had come down with it, including my grandmother. Even their man of business who had come to read the will was infected. Mamma stayed at their home to nurse her mother and sent Papa, Charlie and Tabbie to the nearest inn. But it had already spread there." She took a breath that was nearer a sob. "I can't bear to think about it."

She began to shake and he held her more closely, rubbing her shoulders gently.

"It was weeks before we heard anything. I could not understand why they did not come home. But with so many dead in the village, from the manor to the vicarage, nobody knew whom to ask about my grandparents' other relatives. At last, a neighbour who was a magistrate asked their former steward if he knew who the next heir might be and the man remembered that my parents had a daughter who had not come with them. This magistrate wrote to another in our neighbourhood and he and his wife came to tell us. They were all long buried by then, of course."

"How old were you?"

"Just fifteen."

"And so you were sent to your Grandfather Hassard?"

"Miss Humphreys took me. But he was old and not well."

"That is why he was so eager to see you married."

He felt her nod against his chest. "He wanted me to be safe. But it was a long time before I began to feel safe again. Not until Stanton was born."

"Why was that?"

"Even if you were to die before your father, my son would be Duke. When I became Duchess, I finally began to put down roots here. If you and Stanton were to suffer some misfortune I would have been entitled to the dower house and no-one could send me away."

She had learned too young not only to fear but to expect the worst, he thought sadly. And I was no help to her. But perhaps he could help her now.

"Did you never want to return to your old home, or the homes of your grandparents?"

At this, she raised her head, frowning. "Were they not sold?"

"No. All three estates came to us, two as part of the marriage settlements and the third under your grandfather's will. We immediately let them on twenty-five year repairing leases."

"Why twenty-five years?"

"They are not entailed, and so can be used to establish a younger son or as part of a daughter's marriage portion. It was unlikely they would be required before then."

"How many properties do you have altogether? Apart from here and Gracechurch House, I mean?"

"Six altogether, including the three from your family; the others are a smaller estate in Yorkshire, a shooting box, and a house on Lake Windermere that was left to me by my godfather who died two years ago. It came from his mother whose family had lived there for decades."

"It sounds beautiful. Have you been there?"

"In latter years, when the old gentleman could no longer come to town, I tried to visit him every year."

"Has that been let too?"

"Not yet. I must decide what to do with it. Perhaps you would come with me and advise me?"

Flora sat up and pushed her hair out of her face with both hands. "I'd like that, Jeffrey. Could we take the children?"

"Why not?" He would prefer to have her to himself, but had to accept that her first thoughts were not for him. "Our way could take us near Oakford if you wish to stop at your old home."

"I don't know. Perhaps."

"There is no need to decide now, sweetheart." She looked exhausted. "Come, let us go to bed. May I stay with you tonight—for comfort, nothing more?"

"Comfort?"

"There is a comfort in being together; it is another sort of intimacy. Will you let me give you that tonight?"

He held his breath as she looked at him searchingly. Then he heard, "Yes."

Flora stirred and stretched, enjoying the lazy play of muscles, tendons and joints. She was still sleepy—perhaps she should drift off again. Olivia would breakfast privately with her husband in their rooms. She could understand that—one was not at one's best first thing in the morning when one was enceinte. And they had agreed that while Miss Humphreys would go to church as usual, Miss Mullins, if she preferred, might remain in the schoolroom with the children.

Flora stretched again, tensing her leg and pointing her toe as if about to dance. When she touched another leg, she hastily drew her foot back. Tabbie permitted her to share her bed occasionally, but permission was swiftly revoked if Flora encroached on her sister's side of the mattress.

But Tabbie was dead, wasn't she? Her eyes flew open. Her bedchamber was still dim. The bed curtains were pulled back on one side, and beyond, a rim of light around the window-shutters told her it was past day-break. But why was she lying up against the curtains on the other side of the big bed? She cautiously felt across the sheet until her searching fingers touched warm, muscular flesh sprinkled with hair. She stroked downwards and another hand caught her exploring one.

A male voice said, "Good morning, my dear," then, "Flora?" It sounded concerned.

She turned back towards it, propping herself on her elbow. Beside her, a bulky shape blocked the vestiges of light, then she heard the familiar sounds of a flint being struck and tinder ignited. Tongues of fire licked along the sides of a splint as it was touched to candles whose new flames flickered before steadying to cast a golden light on a familiar face and short brown curls dishevelled from sleep. A name floated into her mind.

"Jeffrey?"

"Who else? You seem unsure."

"I was dreaming. Sometimes I used to get into my sister's bed."

"I see." He seemed to understand for he said no more but slipped his arm around her and drew her down to rest on his chest. He felt warm and his heart beat steadily beneath her ear. Her eyes closed again.

When next she woke, it was to hear, "Your mistress will ring for you when she needs you." His deep voice reverberated inside her head.

"Very good, your Grace." Merle spoke so woodenly that Flora had to stuff the sheet into her mouth to stifle her giggles while the maid withdrew.

"I'm sure she has gone straight to Grimes," she muttered before she could stop herself.

"Do you think so?" She could hear the smile in his voice.

"Probably. And we didn't do anything."

"That can be rectified," he replied, his hand stroking down her back and over her buttocks. She gasped and involuntarily clung closer to him.

"Remember, you need not do anything you do not want to do," he murmured, "but if you would like to explore what could be—don't think, just follow my lead, like dancing. And tell me to wait if I go too fast."

It was not expeditious, but slow and dreamy at first. She couldn't say when he had removed their night gowns, and she felt for the first time the intoxicating sensation of skin to skin. How could a man feel made of satin? Cautiously, she skimmed her palm over him and he lay passive while she explored the planes of his body. Both gasped when she reached his manhood. Hot, hard silk, she thought. He would want to come into her now.

Instinctively, she turned on her back and spread her legs.

But he did not come and lie between them. Instead, he leaned over to kiss her; at first gently, like his good-night kiss, but then deeper, his tongue slipping between her lips and into her mouth. She shivered with excitement and her arms came up to enfold him.

After some time, he raised his head. "Flora, if you wish me to go no further, tell me now."

"Hmmm?"

"Should I stop?"

"No."

"Flora?"

"Don't stop, Jeffrey, please."

"Flora." Her name came on a long sigh. Now she felt his touch—there—and that too was different, and when he came into her, she felt complete. But it was not yet over—she could no longer think. And then she felt his head on her breast, his breath cooling her flesh, while above his hair caressed her. She glanced down and gently brushed the strand back from his forehead, then his lips touched her breast in a soft kiss.

The next time it would be even better, Jeffrey vowed to himself as he kissed his wife.

"Did I—was I?"

He hugged her to him. "You were perfection itself. Did you like it?"

"It was different, strange but nice."

He pressed another kiss to her breast. "That is all that matters."

After some time, she said, "The Fitzmaurices are breakfasting in their apartments. Would you like to breakfast here with me?"

He caught her hand and kissed it. "Above all things."

"Shall we say in half an hour?"

"Excellent," he said again.

"I'll order it. Go now, before I ring for Merle."

Her gaze followed him as he donned his night shirt and dressing-gown and thrust his feet into his slippers. He came back to the bed and stooped to claim another kiss, this time from her beautiful mouth.

"Until later."

Chapter Sixteen

Freshly shaven, Jeffrey pulled on his shirt and trousers and slipped his arms into the blue banyan his valet held for him. "That will be all."

Smiling to himself, he picked up a rectangular parcel and strolled across the saloon to his wife's room. Flora sat at her escritoire writing a letter. To his disappointment, her curls had been tamed and hidden under a lace cap that matched the trimming of her morning dress.

She put down her pen and smiled at him. "Good morning again, Jeffrey."

"I found this for you in Oxford," he said, handing her the parcel.

"Thank you. Oh, it's quite heavy." She placed the parcel on the escritoire and tugged the end of the twine to open the bow knot then carefully unfolded the brown paper. "A book!" She gently touched the gold-embossed brown leather. "What a beautiful binding. Chapman's *Homer*. Is it a new translation?"

"No. It is from the time of Shakespeare, but far superior to Pope, according to the bookseller. It has more vitality, he said."

He stooped to look over her shoulder as she turned the first pages. "How beautiful. And how thoughtful of you,

Jeffrey." She turned her head to smile at him then drew his head down and kissed him, her lips soft on his in this first voluntary caress. "Thank you again. I look forward to our readings, but now come and have your breakfast."

She rose and tucked her hand into his arm to lead him to the table that had been set up at the window. It had rained during the night and the new-washed lawns sparkled in the morning sun, promise of a new beginning. And indeed, he felt new-born. His wife breakfasted lightly on two cups of chocolate taken with a fresh roll split and spread with butter and bitter orange marmalade, but there was a pot of coffee and a plate of ham for him as well as some slices of pound cake.

"Is it enough? I told Merle to be sure there was sufficient for you."

"Thank you. This is ample."

"More coffee?"

"If you please." He passed her his cup. "How are we to entertain our guests today?"

"If it stays dry, I thought we might play bowls after church. I had them prepare the bowling green during the week. We shall draw lots for partners—we are four adults and five children so I'll ask Miss Mullins if she wishes to make up our numbers."

Although the green was at least as old as the Tudor house, Jeffrey couldn't ever remember having played bowls—there had been no one to play against—but he had enjoyed playing cricket at school and at Oxford. "It could be quite diverting, I suppose, especially with the children. Shall we all dine together as we did at Easter? I think we should make that part of our Sundays, whether we are here or in town. We could give the governess and tutor a half-holiday as well so that we can be private."

"That is all very well if they have somewhere to go, like Miss Humphreys who spends Sundays with her brother, but not everyone will have family or friends upon whom they can presume. They cannot be expected to eat with the servants—neither side would like it—but that would mean the kitchen would have to provide trays for them, and that on a Sunday when they should have some rest too. And what of Mr Shorland? He generally dines with us."

"What of us?" he demanded. "Are we never to be private? It occurs to me, Flora, that we pay a high price for our exalted rank and our wealth. Something the meanest cottager can enjoy is denied to us. We play out our lives on stage; our passions and intimacies a comedy to titillate our inferiors. Just think how many people will know by now that I spent the night in your bed and am breakfasting in your room."

She blushed slightly, but then her smile faded. "Your servants—your coachman and groom, your valet—must have known about Meg."

"Yes."

"If they knew, I imagine all the senior ones knew too, even here." She jumped up. "Oh, the humiliation! It's not to be borne!"

"Flora." She backed away as he took a couple of steps towards her. What should he say? Were all his dreams of a new life to be destroyed so soon? Was he to have only one day and night of happiness? What cruel Fate would devise such a punishment?

"Flora," he tried again. "I will not try and excuse what happened; it was inexcusable. But I cannot go back and make it undone. I can only appeal to your generosity and beg you look forward with me—for both our sakes, and for the children. I am in your hands. If you cannot let what is past go, then I must accept your decision but—" He broke off, unable to continue.

She remained rooted before him, silent, impassive, her eyes unfocussed, seeing anything but him.

"As you will," he said submissively.

As he turned to go, she began to shake; seized by fine tremors that set the lace flounces on her robe aquiver. Chalk white, she pressed a hand to her mouth.

"Flora!" In an instant he had swept her off her feet and carried her to the bed where he laid her carefully against the piled up pillows. "Should I ring for your maid?"

She shook her head, raising her hand as she tried unsuccessfully to speak.

Desperate to do something, anything to help her, he poured some of Mrs Fitzmaurice's orange wine and slipped a supporting arm around her shoulders as he held the glass to her lips. To his great relief, she did not reject his offering but sipped at the aromatic cordial.

At last she took a gasping breath, then another deeper one. "I'm sorry."

He shook his head. "You have nothing to apologise for."

"I did not mean to react so harshly. It was the shock—as if I was thrown back in time so that it was happening now, and not many years ago."

"In a way for you it is," he said gently, "but not for those who knew anything then. For them it is old news, long forgotten. And, should they recall it, they will also know there has been nobody since. And never will be. I promise you that, Flora."

"And yet, you would have walked away from me just now."

"Because you wanted me to go, you could not bear even to look at me."

She shook her head. "I was paralysed; I could not do or say anything. I was searching for the right words. I am not as fluent as you." She paused, then added, "It felt as if you were giving me an ultimatum. I should let what is past go, or you will not engage with me in going forward. But I cannot pretend it never happened, or prevent myself from thinking of it. It does not mean that I cannot forgive you. But forgetting is not so easy. It takes time."

He sighed and rested his cheek against the side of her head. "I understand."

She shifted to look up at him. "Could you not have waited another few minutes? When you turned away from me, rebuffed me—"

"I'm sorry. That was never my intention. I felt I must accept your judgement. I still cannot believe my good fortune, Flora. It will take me some time to do so. I have no right to make demands of you."

"If you never ask me anything, how are you to know what my wishes are?"

He smiled. "You are quite right. We need to know each other better. And for that, we need privacy, we need to be able to talk, perhaps even argue, undisturbed."

She smiled back. "Now you have the right of it. See how reasonable we can be? Wait until after May Eve and then I'll see what changes can be made. But now our guests will be looking for us."

He had to be content with that. He would have liked to suggest that they breakfast together each morning but felt it was better not to press her. She still looked very pale. "Why don't you stay at home and rest this morning? I shall escort our guests and the children to church."

"If you don't mind, Jeffrey, I think I will."

"Is there anything I can do for you before I go?"

"Just ring for Merle." Her eyes closed for a moment. "Oh dear, who would have thought being married could be so fatiguing."

"Indeed." He bent and kissed her forehead. "Rest now, my dear."

Mr Fitzmaurice, five children and two governesses, all dressed for church, waited in the hall.

"Where is Mamma?" Tabitha demanded as soon as she saw her father.

"She will not join us today, she is resting."

"My Mamma is resting too," Samuel announced. "We are going with Papa Fitz."

"And with me," Jeffrey said. "Is everyone ready?"

"John, Jasper, remember, keep to the paths at least on the way there," Fitzmaurice called as they set off across the Park, the children running ahead. "How far is it, Duke?"

"On foot, about a mile."

"Excellent. They can shake out some of the fidgets then."

"You apparently had no trouble adapting to your new role as father," Jeffrey remarked.

"No. My mother married twice, so I have a younger brother and sister, although they are older than these, of course. My sister married Hayley last year."

"What, Marwood's heir? He is my cousin—Marwood is my mother's brother."

"So I understand. And Ephraim—my brother—went up to Oxford at the beginning of the Michaelmas term."

"So all the birds have flown the nest. What did your mother say to that?"

Fitzmaurice grinned. "She was distracted by suddenly becoming a grandmother. My elder brother is married but does not as yet have children and suddenly to be presented with three at once, all of whom have plenty to say for themselves, was quite a shock for her. But she took it very well, even begged that we all spend Christmas with them— my stepfather likes to keep it in the old style, complete with yule log and wassail."

"What about Parliament—you have not allied yourself to any party yet?"

"No. It is not generally known, but I do not scruple to tell you that Lutterworth is willing to let me speak and act as I deem fit."

"Is he indeed? He never speaks himself, of course, apart from that one time about the Army estimates and it was clear that his son had put him up to it. Or—Franklin is a friend of yours, is he not? Did you have anything to do with that speech?"

Fitzmaurice shrugged. "I knocked Franklin's thoughts into shape so that he could instruct his father but the earl put his own stamp on it—very effectively, I thought."

"And what stance would you generally take, Fitzmaurice? Are you more Tory or Whig?"

"In general, I am for reform, Duke. Too much is rotten in this state of ours. I wish to be a voice for the voiceless. It can be done—look at Wilberforce and the abolition of the slave trade."

"That was a great day, indeed," Gracechurch said as they reached the church gate where the children waited for them. "Unfortunately, there are not so many of them, although last month saw the repeal of the property tax."

"And who will benefit from the removal of such a direct tax?" Fitzmaurice demanded. "The property owners. But the revenue must come from somewhere and the result will be that indirect taxation will increase, placing a greater burden on the poor."

They had reached the church gate and he broke off to say, "John and Jasper, you may escort your sisters. Samuel, you will go with Miss Mullins."

"Ladies." Jeffrey gestured to the governesses to precede him and he and Fitzmaurice brought up the rear of the little procession.

"What have you done with your ladies?" Lady Ottilia demanded after the service. On hearing that they were resting, she insisted that the Priory party return with her to the dower house for a nuncheon. "I'll send a message to the duchess," she announced. "Tabitha will like to show Miranda the doll's house, I am sure, and I have new marbles for the boys."

Olivia and Flora strolled in the walled garden.

"This time last year, Luke had just gone to Belgium. I did not know if I would ever see him again. So much has changed."

"And for so many families. The Season will be very different this year; so many people are still abroad, then there will be the returning officers, most of whom we will not have seen for some years, and we must not forget those who will never return. It will be hard for their families. Lord and Lady Malvin have aged considerably since Waterloo, according to Gracechurch. I wonder who of our group will be in town."

"Lallie certainly. Her husband has taken his seat and they expect to stay in town for the remainder of the Session."

"It will be good to see her again. But, the way Gracechurch talks, he will expect me to spend more time with him."

"Do you not want to?"

"I think so but I don't want to be dragooned into completely changing my way of life."

"I am sure he will not do that. You must make your expectations clear as well. The fact is, Flora, that both you and I were used to ruling our little kingdoms unopposed, you here and I at Southrode Manor. And when we came to town, we generally did as we wished as far as society was concerned. But true marriage requires us to work in concert with our spouse, to consider his wishes as well as our own. There must be give-and-take. Luke and I review our invitations and decide which ones we will accept, and which we will attend together. We breakfast together, and discuss our plans for the day." She smiled slowly. "And we also make private assignations—evenings when we agree we will not go out and are not to be disturbed. Boudoir evenings, we call them. Cook sends up a supper that we can serve ourselves. We do not dress, that is," she coloured, "I had some dresses made especially for such occasions."

"What are they like?"

"Similar to indoor morning costume but with finer fabric and the neck and bosom are left free, as in evening dress. There is a dressmaker who specialises in such garments; Anthea gave me her direction. Shall I give it to you?"

"Let me think about it," Flora said, wondering would she ever dare suggest such a tryst to Jeffrey. She could imagine how he would respond.

Chapter Seventeen

The guests were invited for nine o'clock. It would be a long night—the May Eve festivities went on until dawn. Jeffrey should be here soon—he wanted them to go down together. He had been most attentive over the past two days, at least as attentive as his duties as host and father permitted. Last night, at her bedroom door, he had framed her face with his hands and just before his lips touched hers, murmured, "May I come to you later?"

At her whispered, "Yes," he had kissed her thoroughly before saying, "Don't let that woman of yours dilly-dally."

His love-making afterwards had been less hesitant, more ardent and Flora found it easy to respond. Afterwards he had remained with her, although with an early breakfast ordered to fortify family and guests for the day ahead, there was no opportunity for repeated indulgence this morning.

"Good evening, my dear."

She smiled at him as he crossed the room to her. "Have you recovered from your exertions?"

"More or less. A day in the saddle would have been less exhausting. But I was most impressed by the way John and Jasper went about it. They were well trained by Rembleton."

"Yes. Stanton used to love to go with him as well. He had so much patience and never talked down to them but always made sure they understood him. If only we could find a tutor or tutors like him for Jasper."

"We shall see. But now," he said as he handed her a jeweller's case, "I saw this in a window in High Street and thought at once of you."

"How kind of you." She opened the leather case and gasped. "Jeffrey, these are exquisite. Thank you!" She carefully lifted the necklace of pearls and pink topaz from its silken bed.

"You wear a lot of pink," he explained. "It suits you."

"This is beautiful—and matching armlets too." She held the necklace against her throat. "I must wear it tonight instead of my pearls. See how it picks up the colour in my gown." She bowed her head. "Will you change them for me, please?"

He came to stand behind her; she could see him in the mirror, head bent, and intent on his task. He carefully unhooked the pearls and drew them away. "Here."

His hand came over her shoulder and she took the pearls, then gave him the new necklace. He set it carefully against her skin, positioning it so that the central cross pendant sat just above the cleft between her breasts. This clasp was trickier and the brush of his fingers on the sensitive skin at her nape sent a ghost of a shiver down her spine.

"There," he said triumphantly and stepped back.

"Oh, it's ravishing—and sits perfectly." She whirled around and threw her arms around his neck, standing on her toes to press an impulsive kiss on his lips. "Thank you."

His arms closed around her, holding her to him. His lips were cool and soft, but they firmed as he returned the kiss. He tasted of Madeira, the smell of the rich wine mingling with the geranium-based scent she had come to recognise as uniquely his. Her hands strayed up to cradle the base of his skull, holding his head to her. Then she lost all thought.

At last he lifted his head. "Flora." His voice was husky and he rested his forehead against hers.

The clock struck the hour, jerking them back to reality.

"We're late," she gasped. "Fasten the armlets—here." She showed him the place between the top of her long glove and her puffed sleeve.

He obeyed, managing quite deftly.

"You make an excellent lady's maid," she quipped.

"Do I?" His eyes gleamed. "If you send yours away later, I'll tend to you."

Flora had never been in the least bit coquettish but now she coupled a sideways glance with a little smile. "Indeed?"

The heavy tapestry that hung inside the massive oak door of the Great Hall had been removed and the door set wide. A bevy of maids spirited away shawls and cloaks before the guests advanced to greet the duke and duchess, and as importantly, one another, eager to see how the elderly had survived the winter and which daughters and sons today entered local society.

When the final tuning of instruments was heard from the gallery, Flora and Jeffrey walked to the centre of the room. "Look up, on the left," she murmured.

Gracechurch smiled to see Tabitha and Miranda peer down over the balustrade, Miss Humphreys standing guard behind them. "Should they not be in bed?"

"They begged to be allowed watch the first two dances."

"What of the boys."

"They were more interested in the jellies Cook made for supper. I promised they could have some later. Jeffrey, what are you about?" she added as he moved to her side, placed his arm around her shoulder, and offered his free hand for hers. "We cannot waltz here."

"Why not? The Fitzmaurices at least will join us and perhaps some others. I'll wager the rest will have a dancing master engaged before the week is out."

Why not? From time to time she had waltzed with him in London but this time putting her arm around him was different, more personal. When she placed her hand in his, his fingers closed over hers in a firm clasp and there was a hum of comments around them. She was dimly aware that Olivia and her husband had joined them, followed by two other couples, but all her attention was focussed on her husband as they began the opening steps. He must have planned it, sent a message to the musicians in advance. He had become adept in surprising her, she thought. The lilting melody lifted and carried them as they swayed and revolved to its voluptuous rhythm and all thought vanished.

Never before had she yielded so to a partner, alert to every movement he made, to every brush of his body against hers. Every change of figure had her on tenterhooks, anticipating a new caress. Now his palm lingered on her hip, now he turned her so that their thighs brushed, now his fingers almost spanned her—not at the high waist-line but below, where her body naturally curved inwards. At times his gaze lingered on her bosom, at others, it met and held hers as if they were dancing a minuet *à deux*. His leg pushed between hers, causing her skirts to stroke her inner thighs with a delicious friction that had her pressing closer, seeking more. But then he turned her away so that they danced hip to hip, facing in opposite directions, but looking back flirtatiously in silent communion. He was extraordinarily inventive in varying the usual turns and holds but she had no difficulty following him. This was dancing of a different degree to any she had ever experienced, reminding her of whispered associations of a gentleman's performance in the ballroom to his prowess in the bedchamber.

She could have waltzed with him forever, but the music stopped. Slightly dazed, she laid her hand on his sleeve and strolled towards the Fitzmaurices.

"You are determined to scandalise your neighbours, I see," Olivia remarked. "Do you think they were ready for that waltz?"

"One must not stand in the way of progress," Jeffrey said solemnly. "I'll lay odds that it will be danced at court before the Season is over."

"Do you think so? I should like to see ladies waltzing in court dress," Flora said, "but I shall not attempt it."

He laughed. "A subject worthy of Rowlandson; I can just picture it. Tell me, would the shock be too much for our neighbours if I were to stand up next with our daughter?"

Flora imagined Tabitha's pleasure and could only say, "No. On May Eve a little latitude may be permitted."

"May it, indeed?" he murmured,

She ignored the wicked glint in his eyes. "She should call *Gathering Peascods*; Miranda knows it too."

Mr Fitzmaurice took the hint. "I'll come with you, Duke; Miranda loves to dance. What about the boys, John and Jasper, I mean?"

"They are at just the wrong age," Flora said.

Olivia nodded agreement. "They are easily discomfited at present."

An amused murmur rippled through the crowd when the two little girls entered the great hall, their small hands resting correctly on their partners' arms. They were pink with excitement as they took their places in the first set.

Sir Frederick Dobson bowed to Flora. "May I have the honour, your Grace?"

"Gladly, Sir Frederick, but, if you will forgive me, not just at once. Mrs Fitzmaurice and I have resolved to watch this time rather than participate. Pray select another lady and I shall be happy to stand up with you for the following dance."

"You wish is my command," he said gallantly and turned to the lady nearest them.

"Has Gracechurch danced with Tabitha before?" Olivia whispered as the dancers joined hands and began to circle.

"Once, after the dancing-master came," Flora replied absently. "He asked what she had learnt and she made him stand up with her there and then so that she could show him."

Olivia began to laugh. "Having decided to change his way of life, he apparently considers all conventions and customs to be fair game. And, of course, because he is a duke who is notorious for his rectitude, none will dare challenge him."

"I fear you are right. He said that those who cannot waltz will have engaged an instructor before the week is out."

"It is very likely. Shall you call for another one? I think you should in case there are some who were reluctant to stand up for the opening dance."

"One more, I think. The first after supper?"

"Excellent. I'll tell Luke. And you should let Gracechurch know. I doubt if he will wish to see you waltzing with another man."

"He must have seen me do so dozens of times."

Olivia shook her head. "That was then. I think you will find his attitude has changed."

"Excellently done, my love," Flora said to a glowing Tabitha. "And now it's time for bed. See, here is Miss Humphreys to fetch you and Miranda. Make your curtsey and say goodnight."

Flora closed her eyes in wonder as Gracechurch bent to receive his daughter's good-night kiss. He might have been doing it all his life, she thought. The leopard can truly change his spots.

Seventeen May Balls lay behind her, thirteen as duchess. Gracechurch's variations for the first two dances had added a little spice to the evening and her confirmation that, yes, there would be another waltz after supper was greeted with some acclaim but now their guests had reverted to their tried and true roles. It was fortunate that May Eve always followed the same pattern and that both servants and guests knew what was expected of them, for tonight, as she moved from group to group, her attention was elsewhere.

Lady Dobson watched Mr Fitzmaurice raise his glass of champagne to Olivia. "I see the latest fashion is for husbands to make love to their wives. I don't know what the world is coming to."

Her neighbour, a spinster of uncertain age tittered. "Surely it is better than devoting themselves to other men's wives?" Her glance at Sir Frederick who continued to dance his way around the younger matrons, caused her ladyship's hand to tighten on her fan.

"Indeed, the times are changing," another lady said. "Parents may no longer make matches for their children—they insist on deciding for themselves. Just look at Princess Charlotte—the Prince of Orange would have been a much better *parti* than an impecunious youngest son from Cobourg, but she would have none of him."

Flora seized on this opportunity to divert the conversation to the upcoming marriage of the Prince Regent's only daughter, heir presumptive to the throne. "I believe the Princess is delighted with her new home in Surrey."

If there were such a thing as a genteel snort, Lady Dobson achieved one. "And well she might be. Sixty thousand pounds to buy the house and land and another sixty thousand to furnish and equip it, all at the state's expense. And they are to have sixty thousand each year between them for their expenses. Leopold has nothing of his own, I know, but is the royal family not to contribute anything? Every other father provides for his daughter himself, but not Prinny."

Another lady sniffed. "Indeed, it is to be hoped that the young couple will be better able to keep household than her father. We are fortunate she is an only child. If there were a brood of sons in his image, the country would be bankrupt."

"The devil makes work for idle hands, be they royal or common," the spinster said. "Do you not agree, your Grace?"

Flora murmured something non-committal and made her escape. Generally, at a ball she and Jeffrey stayed in their own orbits, she in the Great Hall and he in the card room, but tonight he was rarely out of her sight. No matter when she looked, his gaze was fixed on her. When her eyes met his, he made a gesture of acknowledgement—a little nod or quick smile, once he even sketched a quick salute—or had he just brushed back a lock of hair? Anyone watching would say he was flirting with her. She smiled to herself. Lady Dobson would disapprove.

A footman presented a folded paper on a salver. "From his Grace."

She looked around. There he was, in the doorway. What plot was he hatching now? *I understand there is to be another waltz. It is mine. J.* Her pulse quickened as she read his message. When she caught his gaze, he raised an eyebrow. *Understood?*

She smiled and inclined her head, *Yes,* and carefully tucked his note into her reticule.

Supper was served at one o'clock. The benches were moved to the centre of the hall where trestle tables had quickly been set up. As always in the country, where it was the lot of superfluous women to remain at home while their brothers sought adventure elsewhere, there were more ladies than gentlemen and as each lady could not be provided with a squire, the tables were laid with platters of cold meats, tartlets, jellies and cakes so that everyone could help him or herself. Footmen ferried trays of white soup while others poured wine, orgeat and lemonade as desired. Flora passed behind the guests, ensuring that everyone was happy before joining her husband at the high table where her mother-in-law, Mr Harte and the Fitzmaurices also sat.

"It will not be long until Stanton sits here with us," Lady Ottilia observed. "Shall you have a big celebration for his coming of age?"

"Of course, but that is four years away," Jeffrey answered.

"I know," Flora said slowly, "but we should start to consider it now." She looked around. "This is all very well for May Eve but we could not give a proper ball here. Four years gives us time to adapt the house to the current style—add a ballroom, for example, and perhaps, a conservatory. And—could we install proper bathrooms and water closets here like we have at Gracechurch House?"

"An excellent idea. I'll have Shorland make some enquiries. What about a billiard room, if Stanton wishes to invite his friends, as I hope he will." Jeffrey grinned at his wife. "In which case you may prefer to have some bachelor quarters for the young men, especially when Tabitha is older."

"If we are to renovate, let us do it properly," Flora said as she and Jeffrey waited for the second waltz to commence.

"In what way?"

"I do not wish merely to build on a new wing. We should remodel the whole house—open up the rustic and create some pleasant rooms from which one can go directly into the garden. I find the grand staircase so wearying and I don't like to be upstairs all the time. I do not know why I never thought of it before."

He smiled down at her. "I don't think you ever regarded the new house as your home."

"That is true. I have never been comfortable there."

He swung her round to face him. "You made your nest here in the old house. But things have changed, have they not?"

She turned gracefully under his arm, returning to put her hands on his shoulders as he set his at her waist. "Are changing," she corrected him. "I—we stand at a fork in the road. Shall we go on together or separately?"

"Together. Let us create a real home here, Flora, for us and the children."

She looked over her shoulder at him as they began a new figure. "And what about town?"

"There, too, we must change our way of life. I shall still have to go to the House and you will wish to see your friends, but we must make time for each other—and I shall make time for the children too. I promise."

His smile made her want to trace the curve of his lips with her finger; she felt her own lips curve in reply. She instinctively followed his lead, turning to face him and clasping her hands behind her back so that her bosom was thrust forward as his hands rested on her shoulders. She shivered, nipples pebbling, at the slight abrasion of his kid glove on her bare skin. Her breath quickened—she felt the unaccustomed weight of her new necklace at the top of her breasts.

His eyes gleamed and he gently touched the pendant. "Later, I want to see you wearing only this."

"Jeffrey!" She felt herself flush at the intimate murmur. He wasn't flirting with her—he was seducing her.

He laughed softly. Now they were in each other's arms, revolving dreamily to the music. She didn't want the dance to end. And there were still more than two hours until sun-rise. Time to make some last arrangements.

"It's time!"

The great oak door was flung open and the company hurried out into the brightening dawn, the ladies pausing to accept a fine linen handkerchief from one of the maids who stood either side of the doorstep. They scattered busily over the lawns to a chorus of birdsong. Flora paused, listening, as blackbird, thrush, robin and nightingale all fluted their morning challenges, to an accompaniment of chirps, whistles and twitters. The deep cooing of pigeons provided a richer note and—there—she cocked her head at the clear call—yes, it was the cuckoo. Spring was here.

After the stuffiness of the hall, redolent with the heat and smells of a hundred candles and fifty bodies, the crisp morning air was as reviving as champagne. She caught Jeffrey's hand. "Come."

He followed her obediently, skirting the ladies assiduously blotting the morning dew with their handkerchiefs and wiping their faces with the moistened cloths to ensure the beauty of their complexions for another year. She led him through a door in a brick wall into an oblong, walled, flower garden. Neat box parterres were planted with tulips, daffodils and other spring flowers and gravel paths invited the visitor to stroll and admire the shrubs and small trees just coming into leaf.

Jeffrey shook his head in amazement. "I had no idea this was here, and with such a view over to the hills. This is what you meant by being able to step directly into the garden."

"Yes. This has been my refuge," Flora said. "Come to the terrace." She gestured invitingly to one of the chairs that flanked a small table. "I frequently breakfast at the window, but this morning, I thought we might drink to new beginnings."

A wine cooler holding a bottle of champagne stood ready beside two glasses. He picked it up. "Shall I?"

"If you please. Be quick."

Puzzled, he obeyed. As soon as he handed her a glass, she said, "Look to the east."

The sky over the hills was flushed with reds and pinks, and as Gracechurch watched, the crimson disk of the sun rose majestically from behind them, flooding the world with light.

"To new beginnings." He touched his glass to hers, then drained it and set it down.

She put hers beside it and came to him. "Good morning, Jeffrey." Her lips touched his, almost tentatively but as soon as he closed his arms around her and deepened the kiss, she clung to him.

"Come." She led him through the French windows into a charming parlour and from there to a bedchamber that was filled with the morning sun. "Come," she said again, and he went to her. He had come home.

If the Stanton guests wondered why it was the dowager duchess who presided over the hasty pudding and cheesecakes of their May breakfast that year, they were not ill-bred enough to ask. Lady Ottilia appeared to make nothing of the absence of her son and daughter-in-law; if anything she seemed more than happy with the turn of events.

"It is my wish come true," she said to Mr Harte as they returned to the dower house after they had bidden the last guest farewell. "In the beginning, I could not understand why Flora insisted on taking such an interest in her children. I had never questioned that Jeffrey's place was in the nursery—and of course his father would not have heard of his coming to town or my remaining here with him. The Season ran then from November to May and the town air was most insalubrious. It still is, but I suppose May and June when Flora is generally there, it is at its best. However, she stood up to my husband and he let her be, especially after she threatened to emulate the late Duchess of Devonshire—she was still alive then, of course—if he insisted she lead a fashionable life."

Mr Harte chuckled. "No, did she? I can imagine that he gave in."

"After he died, and I saw more of Flora, I came to see that she had the right of it. And after we married, I realised what was lacking in their marriage, but of course it was too late then to do anything for them. I had to accept that I had failed Jeffrey, for he had no expectation of love, at least not within his family."

"It's a wonder she did not take a lover."

"I should not have objected so long as she was discreet, but she had her children and her friends—Mrs Rembleton, in particular. She, too, has had her second chance. I hope they will be as happy as I am."

"As we are," Mr Harte corrected her and kissed her.

Historical Note

This is a work of fiction, but set in a real place and time. While it would be impossible to list all the sources consulted, I wish to mention the following.

For information on Harrow School and The University of Oxford at the dawn of the nineteenth century I am indebted to:

A History of Harrow School by Christopher Tyerman, Oxford University Press, 2000 and

University Life in Eighteenth-Century Oxford by Graham Midgley, Yale University Press, 1996.

The Oxford method of stewing beef-collops on a plate balanced over the backs of two chairs is described in Part II of the 1736 sixth edition of R Bradley's *The Country Housewife and Lady's Director*, published by Prospect Books in 1980.

The £60,000 per annum voted to Princess Charlotte and Prince Leopold after their marriage was split into £50,000 for him and £10,000 pin money for her. According to http://inflation.stephenmorley.org/ £60,000 in 1816 is the equivalent of £4,926,000 in 2017.

The custom of washing the face in May dew at or just before sunrise on 1 May is a very old one; Pepys refers to it in his diaries and in *A Midsummer's Night's Dream*, it is supposed that the sleeping lovers '*rose up early to observe the rite of May*'.

William Hone's *Year Book* of 1832 gives the time of sunrise in England on 1 May as 4.37 a.m. This is GMT and not GMT+1, as in modern Summer-time.

Coming soon: Book One of The Malvin Series

The Potential for Love

"There is an essential something that calls us to another, something that we recognise or that resounds within us on the most intimate level."

"Love, you mean?"

"Rather the possibility or potential for love." Her father shook his head. "It's impossible to describe, Arabella, and it may take us some time to recognise it, but we do know when it is not there."

When Arabella Malvin sees the figure of an officer silhouetted against the sun, for one interminable moment, she thinks he is her dead brother, safely returned against all odds from Waterloo. But it is Major Thomas Ferraunt, the rector's son newly returned from occupied Paris, who stands in front of her. For over six years, Thomas's thoughts have been all of war. Now he must ask himself what his place is in this new world and what he wants from it. More and more, his thoughts turn to Miss Malvin, but will Lord Malvin agree to such a miss-match for his daughter, especially when she is being courted by Lord Henry Danlow?

As Arabella embarks on her fourth season, she finds herself more in demand than ever before. She is tired of the life of a debutante, waiting in the wings for her real life to begin and wants to marry. But which of her suitors has the potential for love and who will agree to the type of marriage she wants?

As she struggles to make her choice, she is faced with danger from an unexpected quarter while Thomas is stunned by a new challenge. Will these events bring them together or drive them apart? Can their potential for love be realised or will it succumb to the first challenge?

A Suggestion of Scandal

England, 1814 If only he could find a lady who was tall enough to meet his eyes, intelligent enough not to bore him and had that certain something that meant he could imagine spending the rest of his life with her.

As Sir Julian Loring returns to his father's home, he never dreams that 'that lady' could be Rosa Fancourt, his half-sister Chloe's governess. Rosa is no longer the gawky girl fresh from a Bath Academy whom he first met ten years ago. Today, she intrigues him. Just as they begin to draw closer, she disappears—in very dubious circumstances. Julian cannot bring himself to believe the worst of Rosa but if she is blameless, the real truth could be even more shocking, with far-reaching repercussions for his own family, especially for Chloe.

Life has taught Rosa to rely only upon herself. Caught up in a shocking turn of events that threaten her with a scandal from which she could never recover, she must save herself even if it means leaving all she loves behind. Can she save her reputation—and her heart?

"A Suggestion of Scandal is a smooth read; providing laughs and gasps in turns. Readers will enjoy the cool-headed Miss

Fancourt, while hoping that Sir Julian puts the pieces of the puzzle together quickly! A host of other loveable and detestable characters keep the entertainment moving through the trials, tribulations, and victories of love." *Historical Novels Review.*

<h1 style="text-align:center">About the Author</h1>

Catherine Kullmann was born and educated in Dublin. Following a three-year courtship conducted mostly by letter, she moved to Germany where she lived for twenty-five years before returning to Ireland. She has worked in the Irish and New Zealand public services and in the private sector.

Catherine has a keen sense of history and of connection with the past, which, she says, so often determines the present. She has always loved writing and is fascinated by people. She loves a good story, especially when characters come to life in a book. But then come the 'whys' and 'what ifs'. She is particularly interested in what happens after the first happy end—how life goes on around the protagonists and sometimes catches up with them.

Writing historical fiction allows her to explore these questions against the background of the early nineteenth century—one of the most significant periods of European and American history. The Act of Union between Great Britain and Ireland of 1800, the Anglo-American war of 1812 and the final defeat of Napoleon at the Battle of Waterloo in 1815 are all events that continue to shape our modern world. At the same time, the aristocracy-led society that drove these events was already under attack from those who recognised the need for social and political reform, while the industrial revolution saw the beginning of the transfer of wealth and ultimately power to those who knew how to exploit the new technologies.

It was still a patriarchal world where women had few or no rights but they lived and loved and died, making the best lives they could for themselves and their children, often with their husbands away for years with the army or at sea. And they began to raise their voices, demanding equality and emancipation.

You will find more information about Catherine on her website www.catherinekullmann.com where she also blogs about Regency facts and trivia in her Scrap Album. Her Facebook author page is fb.me/catherinekullmannauthor